JUST ASH

JUST ASH

SOL SANTANA

carolrhoda LAB

MINNEAPOLIS

Carolrhoda Lab®
An imprint of Lerner Publishing Group, Inc.
241 First Avenue North
Minneapolis, MN 55401 USA

For reading levels and more information, look up this title at www.lernerbooks.com.

Cover image: netsign33/Shutterstock.com.
Design elements: Archiwiz/Shutterstock.com; netsign33/Shutterstock.com.

Main body text set in Janson Text LT Std.
Typeface provided by Linotype AG.

Library of Congress Cataloging-in-Publication Data

Names: Santana, Sol, author.
Title: Just Ash / Sol Santana.
Description: Minneapolis : Carolrhoda Lab, [2021] | Audience: Ages 14–18. | Audience: Grades 7–9. | Summary: "Ash has never thought much about being intersex. But when he gets his period and his parents pressure him to 'try being a girl,' he must fight for who he really is" —Provided by publisher.
Identifiers: LCCN 2020012541 (print) | LCCN 2020012542 (ebook) | ISBN 9781541599246 (library binding) | ISBN 9781728417356 (ebook)
Subjects: CYAC: Intersex people—Fiction. | Gender identity—Fiction. | High schools—Fiction. | Schools—Fiction. | Family life—Massachusetts—Salem—Fiction. | Salem (Mass.)—Fiction.
Classification: LCC PZ7.1.S2633 Jus 2021 (print) | LCC PZ7.1.S2633 (ebook) | DDC [Fic]—dc23

LC record available at https://lccn.loc.gov/2020012541
LC ebook record available at https://lccn.loc.gov/2020012542

Manufactured in the United States of America
1-48118-48770-4/30/2021

FOR EVERYONE WHO HAS BEEN TOLD THAT THEY
ARE NOT ENOUGH EXACTLY AS THEY ARE.
YOU ARE MORE THAN ENOUGH.

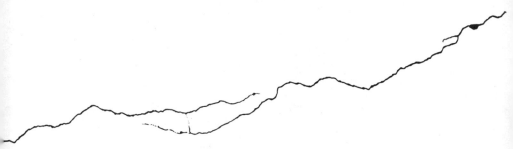

1

As soon as I walked through the front door, I knew there was no escape. Mom hovering in the dining room just beyond the foyer. The wall phone was ringing in the kitchen on my left, but Mom didn't rush to answer it like she usually did. No sign of Dad—yet—but his museum closed early on Wednesdays, so he had to be in the house somewhere. My stomach felt thick and full of ice.

I slammed the door, shutting out the September chill, and dropped my schoolbag. I kicked off my cleats, padding across the hardwood in my socks to stand in the center of the dark-wood dining room, with its oval table and its hanging chandelier. In the 1600s, that monster would've held real candles, and some poor enslaved person probably had to stand on a ladder and light them one by one. Now each socket contained a tiny crystalline light bulb that did nothing to diffuse the natural shadows of the house. It was like being back in colonial times. I took a deep breath to steady myself, inhaling the scents of pine and ash rolling off the thick walls.

"Ash," Mom said, looking hesitantly at me.

Great. Coach must have already called her and told her what had happened today.

Her tightly clasped hands had gone white at the knuckles. The pale roots of her hair were showing where the sandy brown waves were turning gray, catching up to the wrinkles around her mouth.

My name was Ashley. I suspected it was the only name Mom and Dad could agree on when I was born. My sister, Evie, once told me that the doctor had advised them to give me a unisex name, "just in case." When I was born, Dad had been certain I was a boy; Mom and the doctor had been less convinced. Our family physician had explained the basics to me when I was little, but my parents had always avoided talking to me about my body.

Until now.

Dad's voice behind me: "Turn around."

I revolved on the spot, feeling that I had no choice, my stomach tightening instinctively. Dad didn't look like my friends' dads, which had made the fear of him worse when I was growing up. His grizzled gray hair hung down to his shoulders, accentuated by a mean widow's peak. In any other city, he might've been an amateur MMA fighter, maybe a truck driver. Here in Salem, where automobiles were banned on our main street, he co-owned a witch trial museum. It sounded more impressive than it really was. Museums like his were a dime a dozen in this town.

He didn't say anything else, just looked at me. His eyes darkened with disgust. He was close enough for me to smell the alcohol on his breath.

"Oh," Mom cried.

I glanced at her over my shoulder. Her face was buried in her hands. Her T-shirt strained against her heavy frame with every sob.

"Nicole, shut up," Dad grumbled.

I almost agreed with him. It wasn't fair that she was carrying on like this. She wasn't the one who'd been humiliated in front of the entire soccer team, called off the field and made to walk the block and a half home in his blood-stained white uniform.

"Go upstairs," Dad said. "Go change out of . . . that."

I sprinted out of the room, bolting up the staircase. My footfalls on the ancient wood matched the frantic thumping of my heart.

Up in my room, I slammed the door behind me. There was some comfort in its familiarity: the muted gray walls that matched the color of the bedsheets; my gaming computer taking up the whole of my desk space. I used to have a poster of Lionel Messi above my bed until my thirteenth birthday. Now that I was sixteen, a T-shirt from a Skeletronics concert had replaced it. Theta's signature was scrawled across the bottom in big white ink. Meeting the band for a few seconds when I was fourteen was one of my favorite memories.

I pulled off my shirt, then yanked my shorts down, balled them up, and tossed them onto the bed. The seat of my pants was covered in blood.

Why was this happening? I was so angry, I felt tears stinging my eyes. If you knew me, you knew I never cried—not even when I was eleven and accidentally slammed the car door on my hand.

Pulling open my drawers, I tugged on some sweatpants and a T-shirt. *Okay*, I thought. *Calm down. Just calm down.*

The mantra did nothing except make me angrier, and scared. I punched a picture frame off my nightstand, heard it hit the floor and shatter. I knelt on the hardwood, my whole body shaking. This couldn't be happening. This wasn't supposed to happen to me.

A knock sounded on my door. Mom opened it without invitation. She stepped inside, wiping the corners of her eyes with the inside of her wrist.

"I have something that'll help you," Mom said.

She crossed the floor to me and leaned down. In her hand was a small, square, plastic package. I took it from her, not understanding.

"It's a sanitary napkin," Mom said. "For the bleeding."

I looked up at her, feeling dumbfounded and lost.

"Is your stomach hurting?" Mom asked. "Do you have any cramps?"

"Mom," I said, "I'm kind of tired. Can I just lie down?"

"Did you change your underwear?" Mom asked.

"Mom, please?"

Mom hesitated, then backed out of the room. She didn't close the door behind her.

I stared at the crinkling little square in my hand. More than anything, I felt lost.

"Screw this," I said out loud, dropping the pad on the floor. "Screw all of this."

◆◆◆

It wasn't an exaggeration when I told Mom I didn't feel well. I felt so sick that when I lay down, I managed to sleep for three and a half hours. When I woke up, my phone was buzzing wildly on the nightstand. My chest and throat tightened. Unlocking the phone, I scrolled reluctantly through my messages. In my dark room, the glow of the screen was the only light.

dude, said a text from Corey Dietrich. He wasn't on the soccer team but had five different gossip outlets in eleventh grade alone. **wtf?**

I left him on read and kept scrolling.

The most mundane message came from the local library, letting me know I'd forgotten to return *Tituba: A Biography* for the second week in a row. I avoided all the texts from the soccer team, including two from my coach. He probably only cared that he was down a forward right now. Coach Frank could be pretty slow on the uptake.

hey, said a text from Michelle Carrier, my other best friend. **everything okay?**

Shifting, I lay on my back on the bed. I pressed my head against the headboard, running my fingers along the sides of the phone.

I'd first met Michelle when I was thirteen years old, on a middle school field trip to the Freedom Trail in Boston. Matthew Sommerheim called her the N-word and left her in tears. I held her hand, vowing to kick his butt as soon as the teachers weren't around. A few months later, Michelle covered for me when I egged our principal's car as vengeance for his decision to cancel Pizza Fridays. If there was anyone I could trust with what I was going through right now, it was Michelle.

Except I didn't want her knowing about this, did I? I hated this part of me. I'd never hated it before, that was true. But I'd been able to compartmentalize it until today.

nbd, I texted Michelle. **i just got a little hurt during practice. i'll be ok.**

She must be watching TV with her parents right now. It was their corny nighttime ritual, something I liked to tease her about.

is somebody hurting you, ash?

I could see why Michelle would think that. My skin crawled, but I wrote back, **no.**

Michelle wasn't like Corey, and that was why I knew it was safe to talk to her. She knew how to interpret it when I went terse and quiet. When she didn't reply, I felt relieved.

My stomach chose that moment to lurch with hunger. I'd gone to bed without eating dinner. I didn't feel up for a run-in with my parents, but I pocketed my phone and crept down the stairs, taking the creaking steps as quietly as I could. I stole into the kitchen, congratulating myself on my stealth—

And ran straight into my mom. She was sitting at the tiny table in her fuzzy blue bathrobe, hands wrapped around a cup of cranberry juice.

"You don't have to go to school tomorrow," Mom said. "We called the doctor. They can fit us in at eleven."

I didn't know if I was happy about skipping school or apprehensive about the doctor.

"Dr. Howe can make it stop, right?" I said. "The—the blood?"

Mom nodded. I didn't like the way she looked at me. Like she barely recognized me. Who was I, and what was I doing here? Where had her actual son gone? I felt a fresh wave of fear. I wanted her to tell me that things would be okay, that we could go back to the way everything was before.

She averted her eyes, sipping her juice.

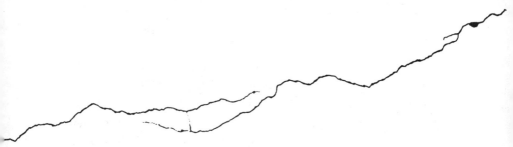

2

When I got out of bed in the morning, I stepped on broken glass. Cursing up a storm, I sat down and picked the tiny shards out of my foot. Blood ran from the shallow wounds, thin and watery, until I pressed my pillowcase against them. I was getting sick of the sight of blood.

The photo I'd knocked over the night before was the only one of my sister and me. I scooped it off the floor and sat looking at it, lost in thought. I was ten in the photograph; Evie was nineteen. Frozen in time, we stood in Lappin Park on Essex Street. We were posing in front of that statue of Elizabeth Montgomery astride her broomstick, our arms around each other's shoulders. That day, Evie had said it was funny that the town most famous for executing suspected witches embraced all things occult now. It was a total one-eighty, she said.

I put the photo on my nightstand, pulled my pajamas off, and strode across the bedroom to open the closet door. The mirror on the inside lit up when I pulled the drawstring light. Normally I spent approximately zero percent of my time thinking about my appearance, but all things considered, maybe that should change. I looked pretty unremarkable—scrawny, dark-haired, strong shoulders, tanned skin. I had pecs and pubes. If my hair had been longer, I would have looked less like a prettyboy and more like a tomboy. You could only really see my Adam's apple when I talked.

What was really different about me was between my legs. My penis was small, about four inches. Instead of balls, it hung over a pair of tight vaginal lips. I'd grown up with them, never giving them extra thought before now. It wasn't like they did much of anything. I pissed the other way, from my dick, which I'd properly acquainted myself with when I was twelve years old and found out how good girls looked in two-pieces.

A sharp pain shot through my stomach. I ran as fast as I could to the bathroom, scared of bleeding through my pants.

A few minutes later, I was downstairs in the kitchen, sitting at the table with Dad, watching Mom scramble eggs. It was hard to have an appetite this early in the morning, especially for something so greasy. I wondered whether Dad was coming to the doctor with us. He didn't say. After sopping up his eggs with a slice of bread and shoving it in his mouth whole, he got up and left without a word. I guessed that meant he wasn't coming with us. I didn't want him there, anyway.

After breakfast, Mom and I walked up Summer Street, where we'd lived my whole life. The houses like mine were old and gray, with splendid gates standing out front. Little prefabricated junks stood between them, cheaply made houses that hadn't existed until the past twenty years. They cost less to move into but went up in flames every time there was a lightning strike.

Just before Summer Street turned into North Street, we turned onto Essex, where cars were banned. The road was so picturesque that it might as well have popped out of a Norman Rockwell painting. The sidewalk was entirely brick and lined with stooped green trees, though a few of the leaves were curling at the edges and turning yellow. Once, the street's main attractions might have been silos and pillories. Now the storefronts with their unlit neon signs advertised knickknacks and talismans, tarot readings, crystal wands to bring out your inner witch. I'd never quite worked out how much of the flair was genuine and how much was catering to the tourists. Come October, our little town was going to be swamped with them.

Mom and I ended up on Bridge Street, along the river. My favorite restaurant, the Pickled Pearl, was open for business. A giant fake crab sat on the weathered roof, fishing rod clutched between its pincers. The restaurant looked out of place between the historically unchanged houses on either side of it, two- and three-story residences, all dark gray—a color the Puritans apparently had had a real hard-on for. The chimneys were jammed in the centers of the roofs, which was the style back in the day. The windows were round and latticed underneath the pointy gables, hanging modillions dripping like gingerbread icing. The Puritans were supposed to be all about the simple life, but their houses definitely didn't reflect that philosophy. Years later, the descendants who had inherited them, my family included, didn't seem to mind their forebears' hypocrisy.

You could cross all of Salem by foot in twenty-five minutes. It didn't take us long to reach our destination. The doctor's office was in a flat building across the street from the Satanic Temple. I'd been going there for checkups since I was in kindergarten. Most of the other patients were still small. When we walked into the waiting room, there were two toddlers playing with the train set on the floor. The seats were big, multicolored Lego blocks, a circus mural on the wall. I considered grabbing a toy car and joining the kids, but I didn't have to. A nurse called my name mere minutes after we sat down.

"Mom," I said when we got to the exam room, "could I do this alone?"

Mom looked at me in shock. "You don't want me here?"

Of course I didn't.

"Let's give Ashley a minute to change into a gown," said the nurse.

That taken care of, I sat on the exam table, which was covered in a sheet of paper. Eventually the door opened again and two people walked in—Mom and the doctor.

I stared. "You're not Dr. Howe," I said.

A lady in her late forties smiled at me. "I'm Dr. Tran," she said. She had a triangular, pointy face framed by very straight hair. "You don't have to worry; Dr. Howe handpicked me to replace him."

I must have been staring at Dr. Tran while I waited for instructions, because her smile flickered. I'd been told before that my default face was kind of cold-looking. I couldn't help it if I'd been designed that way.

Dr. Tran listened to my heart and lungs with a stethoscope, though I didn't know why that was necessary. Then she sat at her table and looked at the information on her computer screen.

"So," she said, "I see here you have congenital adrenal hyperplasia."

"What?"

"That you're intersex."

"Yeah."

"Is that why you've come in today?"

"I'm bleeding," I said. The thick cotton pad felt uncomfortable in my boxer briefs.

"And you're sixteen?" Dr. Tran asked.

"Yeah."

"It's inconvenient," she said, "but consistent with what we know about your condition. Most girls with CAH experience irregular periods. Sometimes menarche arrives late, or it never arrives at all."

Most girls? What? "I'm a guy," I said, bristling.

"Well, I think it's best not to make any assumptions right now," she said, in a tone that implied she was doing exactly that. "I'm going to have the technician draw some blood today."

"Why? Why is that necessary?"

"We may be able to determine if you're fertile. There's a good chance of that now."

"I'm not," I said. "Nothing comes out when I—"

I stopped there, not really wanting to talk about private habits.

"I don't mean your phallus," Dr. Tran said, apologetic. "You have at least one functioning ovary. That's where the menses is coming from right now. That means you may be able to reproduce vaginally."

What the actual fuck was she talking about? "Take it out," I said desperately. "I don't want it."

"Ashley," Dr. Tran said, "I can't do that."

"Why not?" None of this was making sense.

"You're too young for an invasive surgery of that nature," Dr. Tran said. "You might change your mind when you're grown up and decide you want to have children."

I stared at Dr. Tran, feeling weirdly violated. She just wasn't getting it. "I'm a guy," I repeated.

"You might change your mind about that later," Dr. Tran said.

How did you change your mind about something that was objectively true? I couldn't change my mind one day and make fire feel cold, or make my dad have a personality. While I was wondering how such a thing was done, Dr. Tran told me to get dressed and go next door for a blood test. I did, but I was in such a stupor; I might as well have sleepwalked there. Suddenly nothing I thought or felt mattered anymore, even when it came to my own existence.

◆◆◆

Dinner was quiet that night. Nobody said a word at the table, forks scraping on plates as we cut up our salmon doused in lemon butter. I asked to be excused early, and neither of my parents stopped me.

Upstairs in my bedroom, my stomach was in knots. Mom hadn't said anything about my staying home again tomorrow. That meant I was going to school. I'd have to face a jury of my peers. Who knew what they'd been saying about me today? If I was lucky, the damage wasn't totally irreparable. It all depended on whether I could control the narrative about me.

Michelle would be there. If nothing else, she could always make me laugh. But what happened when she wanted to know what my problem was, like everyone else did? I couldn't hide from her forever. It was a real shame too. Hiding was all I wanted to do anymore.

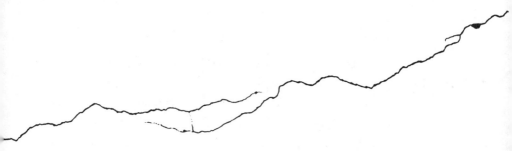

3

Deodat Lawson High School was a public school. Like so many things in Salem, it took its name from a prominent player in the witch trials. If not for old Deodat, who was a minister here in the late 1600s, we wouldn't have a firsthand account of the accusations. History owed him for setting the record straight. To me, his name was most notable for that time in sophomore year when I sneaked onto the school lawn at night and vandalized the sign out front. *Deodab Lawdank High School*, it read for four days. The week's suspension was worth it.

The high school didn't fit in with the architecture around it. It was made of sunny yellow brick, violating the unspoken law that all buildings in Salem be gray or brown. I shouldered my schoolbag and walked inside. The entrance hall was covered in dizzying black-and-white tiles like a checkerboard. On my immediate left, trophies in shining display cases immortalized the victories of athletes gone by. Mine was going to be among them one day, if I had any say in it.

I took a right into the corridor where the eleventh-grade lockers were housed. They were all an unnatural shade of blue, like the sky as envisioned by a first grader having a fever dream. I stopped in front of my locker and spun open the combination lock. Lost in the throng of students, I wasn't attracting any weird looks. Not yet, anyway.

Corey Dietrich rushed over to me. He was a skinny guy, rail thin; even his pink sweatshirt couldn't provide him with artificial bulk. He wasn't wearing pink on purpose. He had a kind of color blindness that made it hard for him to tell shades of red apart. Everybody liked to say that Corey came from a hillbilly family. I'd been friends with him since fourth grade, so I knew his parents were accountants, but I could see how he got this reputation. One of the teeth on his bottom row was bent the wrong way. He'd worn his scraggly blond hair down to his shoulders until the second week of school this year, when he'd taken a pair of safety scissors to it, and the chop job wasn't doing him any favors.

"Dude, what the actual hell?" Corey said.

"Hey," I said.

"Evan Carmichael said you were, like, *bleeding*," Corey reported, just in case I wasn't there when it happened. "You got your period!"

"Guys don't get periods, Dietrich," I said. "Grow up, would you?"

Evan Carmichael himself slithered over to us. I knew him from the soccer team, where he played center back, because he wasn't good enough for forward. I hated the elfish look about him, the upturned nose and pointy chin, the too-big front teeth that suggested some clandestine lagomorph ancestor. Those chompers always made it look like he was getting ready to bust a lung laughing.

"You get your period, Bishop?" Evan asked casually.

"Nah," I said. "Must've just tripped and fallen on your microdick."

I heard a couple of sycophantic "oof"s from the nearby crowd. Evan found it funny too—or maybe it was just the rabbit teeth making it look that way. I hurried to class before he could get another word in. If I stayed evasive for the rest of the day, this entire thing ought to blow over.

I didn't have any morning classes with Michelle, so I didn't get to see her until lunch. Our cafeteria had restaurant-style tables, small and round and scattered every few feet. After I got my food, I found Michelle sitting alone at our usual table, waiting for me. When she saw me approaching, she flashed a wide smile that dimpled her cheeks, white teeth brilliant against her dark skin. Her tight, light brown curls skimmed her shoulders today, though she often wore her hair in a knot— more convenient for ballet. She had a habit of pursing her heart-shaped lips when she thought deeply, which made her Cupid's bow scrunch up. She did that when I sat down, so I knew she was thinking about recent events.

But all she said was, "Did you see the anime club's already recruiting? They're playing *Spirited Away* next month. They say it's a really good movie."

"Weebs," I said.

"Hush, you."

Then we started talking about the Skeletronics, our favorite band. Most weekends, one of us visited the other's house, and we blasted their discography for hours. We were arguing over which song was better, "Love Me for My Circuits" or "I Became a Robot through Osmosis," when Louisa Carmichael stopped by our table, clearing her throat and tucking her straight red hair behind her ears.

"I want to talk to you," Louisa said.

"I'm busy," I said. Louisa and I had dated for five months in tenth grade. I wasn't interested in the love-you-hate-you dance anymore.

"You lied to me," Louisa said.

"What are you talking about?" I asked, exasperated.

"You're a girl!" Louisa said. "You fucking lied to me!"

She wasn't causing a scene—not yet, anyway—but she tended to, if you gave her the time. The tables near ours hushed up.

"I'm not a girl, Lou," I said quietly.

"You got your period," Louisa said. "Evan told me!"

"I didn't get my period!"

"What was that, then? Guys don't bleed like girls do! You're a dyke, aren't you?"

"What?" My head spun.

"You tricked me so you could get with me. You think I won't warn everyone else about you, sicko?"

"Louisa," Michelle said quietly. "Maybe you should stop."

Louisa turned on her. "What, so you're defending *him? Her?*"

"I don't think he did what you're saying he did. And you're basing it all off of what someone else told you, anyway. Just take it down a notch if you want to have an actual conversation with him."

Apparently this suggestion didn't appeal to Louisa. She shot me one more dark look and retreated from our table, but the damage was already done. The people nearest us were staring. I mashed up my potatoes with my fork, just to give myself something to do.

Michelle put her hand on top of mine. A tiny wrinkle creased her forehead. Her glasses slid down her nose.

"It's nothing," I muttered. "I swear."

Michelle let go of me, making my hand feel cold. The rest of me felt cold too.

What I was really dreading was soccer practice. The team met every Wednesday and Friday after school in the field around the block. It had its own locker room and showers in a small, square building off the pitch. That afternoon, when I stepped onto the grass in my cleats, a couple of heads turned my way, faces bearing smirks. Nobody said anything to me, so I thought it might blow over still.

Coach Frank, squat and round and gray-haired, stood with his hands on his hips and his legs spaced apart. He looked nervous. Coach pretty much always looked nervous, so I didn't read too much into it. When most everyone had gathered on the field, he blew his whistle and made us warm up for drills.

It was a regular afternoon in every respect. After we cooled down, it was time to shower. I stayed on the field, stalling, bending down to tie up my laces. In the locker room, you kept your eyes to yourself. If you happened to catch a glimpse of something, it was fine, but look too long and you'd be branded gay for the rest of your high school career. Here at Lawson, at least, that was still considered an insult. So I'd been able to dodge scrutiny before. But a lot of the guys were giving me strange looks today. Going in the locker room with them would be disastrous. I decided to hightail it home.

I stalked over to the bleachers on the side of the lawn, where I'd left my gym bag. The goalkeeper, Jay Tulley, followed me. The setting sun beat angry patterns off his flattop hair.

"Hey," he said. "Hey, why aren't you showering?"

"Got places to be," I said, shouldering my bag.

If it was just him, I could have dodged the bullet. But Matthew Sommerheim and Ryan St. Paul had joined him. Why were those three socializing? They hated each other's guts.

"You don't want to show us your pussy?" Jay asked.

"Show us your pussy, Bishop!"

"You know he's got both, right? I saw, once. He uses the urinal."

"Show us your pussy!"

These guys were my teammates. I couldn't believe they were treating me like this. My tightly wound nerves combined

17

with my smart-ass mouth to make me say something I instantly regretted.

"Why? Am I the closest you'll ever get to one?"

I ran. I ran from Gedney Street to Norman Street, my heart bursting in my chest. The glare of the sunset burned my eyes, red-hot, molten gold. I was still running when I hit Charter Street. I ran past the five-story apartment buildings crammed unnaturally beside the sprawling cemetery with its wrought-iron gate, where at least three of the famous witch trial victims had been laid to rest. I slowed down, rubbing a stitch in my side. As I walked on, the modern pavement gave way to a sidewalk of ancient brick and beat-up stone.

There were words carved into the stone, the letters soft at the edges where time wore at them.

"On my dying day, I am no witch."

"God knows I am innocent."

"Oh Lord, help me!"

They were the last words of Sarah Good, Elizabeth Howe, and Rebecca Nurse, three of the women killed on witch-craft charges in 1692. This was our town's memorial to them. Beyond the engravings was a grassy quadrangle filled with locust trees—the same type of tree from which they had been hanged. The trunks were almost black, thick and grooved, forking into dozens of waxy-leafed branches.

The first woman killed on witchcraft charges was named Bridget Bishop. She probably didn't commune with the devil, but she was a seventeenth-century oddity in another way. Independently wealthy, she owned not one but two taverns. Her third and final husband was rich in his own right: he was a sawyer, and everybody needed lumber in those days. So Bridget stood to inherit even more from him once he died.

People hated Bridget Bishop. She owned a big house full

of cats and poppets. She violated the unspoken dress code by wearing red from time to time. When a man argued with her, she did the unthinkable and argued back. She was too different, see, too freakish. She just had to be a witch.

Her neighbors dragged her to court on June 10. They stripped her down, right there in the courtroom, let everyone gawk at her as she sobbed and covered herself with her hands. She had a third nipple. See that? She had to be a witch. Normal people looked one way or another. There was no room for variation. If you found someone who didn't fit, it was safe to throw them to the dogs.

Bridget Bishop was my ancestor on my dad's side. Her neighbors killed her that day in June, but now I felt as if a part of her lived on in me. She might even have been reborn in me, if you believed in such a thing. Maybe her vengeful spirit had cursed me to live the way she had. She was peering out through my eyes at the world around her that had changed in so many ways, but not nearly enough. How would it treat her now? What could I do to avoid a fate like hers?

I sat on one of the crumbled stone benches facing the quadrangle. Bridget's final words were written on the ground with the other victims'. Three centuries later, they spoke out to me in warning. "You will keep silent," they said.

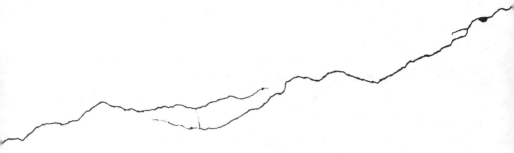

4

That Saturday was the most boring Saturday in recent memory. I wanted to visit Michelle's house, but I didn't want to sit there with her knowing she was thinking things about me. For the first time ever, I finished all my homework, just to take my mind off my dwindling social prospects. I checked my messages, deleting the ones from the soccer team. There was one email I couldn't ignore. It came from Dr. Tran, and it looked like she had written it late at night on Friday. She'd sent it to my account, but seemed to have mistaken it for my family's account.

This was what it said: "Ashley's blood cells have low amounts of FSH, which means she may be able to reproduce when she comes of age. A vaginoplasty would have to be performed to widen the birth canal. With androgen blockers and a full penectomy, she would be virtually indistinguishable from a non-intersex female."

I mashed the Delete button. The thought of some guy knocking me up made me feel like I was going to puke. My throat went tight with panic. Everybody talked about me like I was some abstract concept: barely even sentient, incapable of taking offense.

On Sunday, my self-imposed exile got on my nerves. I needed to hang out with somebody. For some reason, I still couldn't bear to know what Michelle was thinking, so I texted Corey and asked if he'd like to bike down to the Salem Willows. His response, when it came, wasn't as enthusiastic as it usually was.

uh

yeah i guess

Beggars weren't choosers.

I rode my bike up Summer Street and onto Lynde Street, slowing when I passed Gallows Hill with its crooked, creepy locust tree. According to local lore, accused witches had hung from it once. In a few weeks' time, the locals would hang cobwebs and animatronic skeletons from it instead.

The Salem Willows in the east of town was our only beach. Anyone picturing sun-bleached dunes and waves ripe for surfing was in for a rude awakening. The lumpy, cream-colored sand was dotted with dozens of weeping willow trees, green and gold tresses hanging from flexible, droopy branches. I hopped off my bike and walked it down the road to the shore. The sea was periwinkle, flecked with pink patches where the autumn sun paid it too much attention. Pedestrians in windbreakers walked beside the water. Down south, past the bed of rocks full of nesting, noisy seagulls, was a pizza place. I ate there sometimes, although their pie was kind of doughy.

"Yo," Corey said, pulling his bike up beside mine. "What's up?"

"Not much," I said.

We hopped on our bikes, cycling toward the pizza place. Corey was always hungry, and I was pretty sure he was about to wheedle me into buying him a slice. He surprised me by stopping halfway down the path, little clouds of sand kicking up under his bike tires when he put his foot down. I was forced to stop too.

"I, uh," he said, "I'm not gay. You know that, right?"

I raised my eyebrows at him. "Congratulations."

"No," he said quickly. "See, you—they're saying you're a girl, but like . . ."

I was so aggravated that I let my bike fall to the ground. I didn't even care about the sand getting in the chains. "I'm not a fucking girl, Dietrich!"

"Hey, hey!" Corey yelped. "What's the matter with you? Look, what's going on?"

It felt ridiculous to talk about this in the middle of the beach—lazy long-legged birds standing in the shallows, bills gliding under the water as they fished for lunch. The ocean roared in my ears like a distant crowd. The prickling spray was cold.

"I'm both," I said.

"Huh?"

"Both," I yelled above the surf. "I'm both. They couldn't tell what I was when I was born, okay? Still can't, kind of. But they brought me up like a guy, and that's what I am. I'm a guy."

Corey's eyes widened. "I didn't know you could be both," he said. He was speaking at room volume; if I hadn't watched his lips, I would have missed it.

"It's rare," I said. "But yeah. You can."

"What about, like, chromosomes or whatever?" I could tell from his frown that he was struggling to remember our freshman year biology class.

I shook my head. "It's not that simple for someone like me." I hoped he wouldn't ask more follow-up questions. I honestly didn't know what my chromosomes said I was, or if it even mattered. I vaguely remembered Dr. Howe telling me it wasn't always as clear-cut as XX = girl and XY = boy, but I'd never been entirely sure what that meant.

"You gonna make a big thing out of this?" I asked Corey.

"Nuh—no."

"Good," I said. "You wanna bike to Michelle's house?" If Corey was with me, he'd be so busy running his mouth off about everything else under the sun, she might forget for a little while that something was wrong with me.

"No, man," Corey said. "I still want pizza. I haven't eaten since breakfast."

"It's eleven o'clock," I said.

"Yeah, that's what I mean."

We walked our bikes to the pizza place and chained them up outside. Inside, it was way too warm for the start of autumn. Doughy pie or not, Pizzazz Pizza was kind of neat. The front counter, where you placed your order, was a glass display case full of stuffed dolls and laminated comic books. They were prizes; if you won enough tickets from the pinball machines, you could trade for them. Downstairs was the creepy catering hall where I'd had my eighth birthday party, with walls made up like puzzle pieces. I remembered crying when the costumed mascot posed for a photo with me.

Corey and I put our orders in and sat down at a booth with cracked leather. He drummed his fingers on the table, but I wasn't bothered. He'd always been a restless ball of energy. At one point, he got up to play a couple of rounds of *Pac-Man*, leaving me alone to watch videos on my phone. He finally sat his skinny ass down when our order was ready, beaming at me with all his teeth.

I wasn't hungry. I ate half a slice of pizza and he finished it for me. He finished his too. We walked outside, talking about a test we were pretty sure we had both failed.

We were unlocking our bikes when he reached over and grabbed my chest.

I shoved him so fast, it could only have been a reflex. "What the fuck are you doing?"

"Hey—hey, I'm sorry!" he said quickly. "I just wanted to see if you had tits. You don't, but—"

"Give me one good reason I shouldn't beat the shit out of you!"

"I'm sorry! I was just curious!"

I was so angry that I couldn't think straight. My fists were shaking. Somehow I managed to steady them long enough to climb on my bike.

"You can delete my number from your phone, you piece of shit," I said.

I couldn't believe all the years I'd wasted being Corey's friend. I wished I could take back every time I'd let him borrow my Netflix password or leech off my Wi-Fi. I tore off across the beach, the sand rising around my face. I was starting to feel like my body didn't belong to me anymore. It scared me.

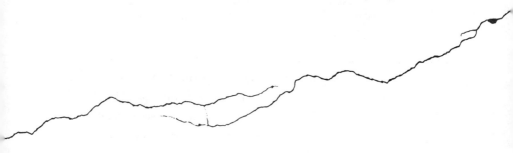

5

Oh, God. It was happening again.

I was leaving math class and heading to English when I stopped short in the middle of the hallway. Something hot and wet had filled my underwear, chilling quickly on my skin.

I ran at breakneck speed to the guys' restroom, locking myself in a stall. I pulled a sanitary napkin out of my book bag, where it had been waiting since last month, and frantically ripped into the plastic packaging. My eyes were blurry. I told myself I wasn't crying. I put the pad on, attaching the sticky side to my boxer briefs, and pulled my pants back up. No one had been in the restroom when I'd entered, but now, when I exited the stall to toss away the plastic wrapper, Evan Carmichael was standing by the sink. He turned around, raising his eyebrows at me.

"What's that?" he asked.

"Shut up," I said, tossing the garbage in the bin.

"Shouldn't you be using the girls' room now?" Evan asked. His mouth curled at one corner.

"You mean this isn't the girls' room? What're you doing here, then?"

I shouldered my way out the door and into the hallway. At which point my lower gut chose to cramp so badly that my knees went weak. People looked at me when I passed them, as if they could somehow tell what kind of pain I was in. I wished that were true. Maybe then they would have empathized and laid off. Then again, what miracle was I expecting? This was high school.

Over the next few hours, the stares became so unbearable that at lunchtime, I ate outside, sitting on the front steps. The only other kids out here were the drama geeks, furtively sneaking cigarettes and sighing over how grown up they were. I picked at my sandwich with no appetite. I heard the heavy doors swing open and scrape shut. Michelle came down the steps and sat next to me.

"Corey told me you guys are fighting."

"That's what he said?" Leave it to Corey to turn sexual harassment into a mutual disagreement.

"Ash," Michelle said, looking at me intently, "You wanna tell me what's going on?"

I looked away, watching a driver across the street pop open the hood of his car. I said, "It's true, what they're saying about me. I'm both."

"It's true?" Michelle asked. "That you're intersex?"

I nodded.

"That doesn't mean you *are* both," Michelle said. "That means you *have* both."

She was the first person who saw me the way I really was. I looked at her, wishing I could live in her eyes instead of the real world.

Her lips scrunched up. She whispered, "Did you get your period last month?"

I nodded.

"Do you have it again this month?"

"How did you know?"

"It's kind of a monthly thing, Ash."

"How do I stop it?"

"You don't," Michelle said. "Except . . ."

"Yeah?"

"I think some kinds of birth control can stop it."

"My parents would never sign off on that," I said. As wacky as Salem might have become in the years since the hangings, my folks were as conservative as old Judge Hathorne himself. Why would I need birth control, they'd argue, if I wasn't having sex? And of course I wasn't having sex. Teenagers did not have sex. They were innocents, hardly anything like human entities with natural urges.

Michelle paused. "What if we went to Planned Parenthood? There's one in town, I think. You can get birth control there without your parents knowing. They have to give it to you; it's the law."

"I don't know where it is," I said.

"I'll find it on my phone. We can sneak there after school. Just tell your parents you're hanging out with me. They won't ask any questions."

It was hard not to stare at her just then, analyzing every minute detail of her profile. "You don't think I'm a freak?"

"No," Michelle said. "Well—there's one thing that's bothering me . . ."

"What?"

"Why didn't you ever tell me about this?"

"You need to ask? Look how everybody else is treating me."

Michelle looked hurt. "I'm not everybody else, Ash."

If anyone could make me feel ashamed of myself, it was her. "I just didn't want you looking at me any differently."

She wasn't. She had the same warm spark in her eyes she'd always had.

"I'm friends with you because you're Ash," Michelle said. "Not because of the shape of your pee-pee."

I broke into the first grin I'd worn in a month. I slugged her shoulder, because I knew she could take it, even if she let out an exaggerated "Ow!" and swooned dramatically.

"After school," Michelle said. "We're doing this."

She was as good as her word. She waited for me on the front lawn when the bell rang. We walked back to my house so I could get my bike out of the shed. It had pegs on the back of it, so when I climbed on the seat, Michelle stood on the back, her hands on my shoulders. We took off down the road, Michelle reading directions to me from her phone.

When I pedaled down Derby Street, the white girders of Salem Harbor Power Station came into view, dwarfing the fishing piers along the weedy bay.

"Are you taking me to get electrocuted?" I asked.

"Now you know," Michelle said. "It's all a ploy to keep this bitchin' ride to myself."

Beyond the power plant was the Planned Parenthood building. The gray cement of the structure made it look a little bit like a prison. Probably the camouflage warded off annoying protesters. There was one sitting outside anyway, a humorless old lady in a folding chair. *BABY MURDERERS!* read the sign on her lap. It must have taken a lot of effort and energy to sit there stewing in her own meanness; she was nodding off.

Michelle hopped off the bike, stretching and swinging her arms, like she had done all the work and was beat. When she was wearing that dopey little smile, it was hard to tell her to knock it off.

On the inside, the building looked like your typical doctor's office. Michelle and I went up to the front counter, where a receptionist with a perky blond ponytail asked what we were here for today.

"Birth control," I said.

She looked at Michelle. "Oh, do you have a student ID?"

"Um," Michelle said sheepishly, "not for me." She jerked her head at me, then inched away for emphasis.

Color shot to the poor receptionist's face like somebody had spattered her with rosy pastels. "Oh!" she said. "Oh, of course, I'm so sorry! Right this way, please."

An hour later, I had a seven-dollar monthly prescription for some pill with ingredients called ethinyl estradiol and levonorgestrel. What a freaking mouthful. The physician said if I remembered to take it every day, it'd stop my little problem for a whole year. I couldn't believe it had been that easy. Michelle whooped with victory as I unlocked my bike.

"No more periods for you!" Michelle said.

"I never would've thought of coming here," I said. "I could kiss you."

"D'aww," Michelle said, grinning broadly. She made a joke of it, but there was a hint of pink to her smooth brown cheeks.

"Let's go back to my place and listen to some Skeletronics," I said. "We'll play 'Metal Girl in a Fleshy World' until we get sick of it."

"We never get sick of it," Michelle said.

"Truth."

"I wish the Skeletronics would come tour here! Sure, they're supposed to be robots, but they're skeleton robots! It fits their aesthetic! You'd think they would!"

"Maybe they don't want to get caught up in all the side-show drama of Salem." Case in point: The Halloween parade on Salem Common was coming up soon. Every year, it was a guaranteed freak fest. I felt weary just imagining what antics the paraders would get up to this year. One year, there were a bunch of simulated decapitations right there in the square, even

though nobody in the history of Salem had ever been decapi-
tated. A guy had been crushed to death by stones, though.
"More weight!" Giles Corey had demanded, refusing to admit
he was a witch.

Pretty badass, I thought. I hoped my last words would be
that memorable.

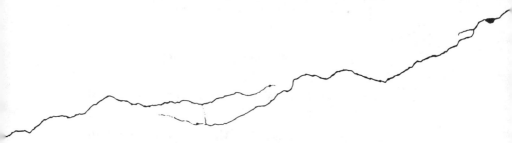

6

In the days following my excursion with Michelle, I started to feel better. The lady at the clinic had warned me the pills could take a week to start working, but it didn't matter. Just knowing I'd go back to normal soon gave me something to look forward to.

But the world was continuously conspiring against me, as I found out during Wednesday's soccer practice.

"Ash," Coach Frank said nervously. I'd only just set foot on the pitch. "Can I—uh. I need to talk to you."

I followed Coach Frank away from the white chalk lines, stopping when we hit the bleachers. His waddling walk made me wonder if he was suffering from some poorly healed hip injury.

"You're off the team," Coach said in one breath.

"What?" I burst out.

Coach's eyes bugged with fear. "Shh, shh," he said, twisting his hands in his shirt. "This is the boys' soccer team—"

"And I'm a boy!"

"It wasn't my decision," he said. I knew he was lying. Confrontation scared him.

"Then whose was it?" I prompted.

Coach hesitated. "We've had some phone calls . . . concerned parents. They don't like knowing that their kids—"

"What?"

"They don't want a girl on the boys' soccer team. You have to understand that . . ."

I didn't wait to hear what else he had to say. I turned around and marched off the field.

When I got home, I felt miserable. Mom wasn't home yet; in October, she always got super busy, taking tourists to see Pioneer Village and the House of the Seven Gables. I heard noise in the living room and went in to find Dad sitting there, watching TV.

It was as grand a living room as there had ever been—a huge, unlit stone fireplace in the wall and a cellar door where spare kindling might have been kept once. The wooden ceiling rafters were bare, which made the room look even bigger than it was. Dad spread his knees like a slob, a beer in hand. After I changed out of my kit, I went in there and sat down with him. I was surprised to find him home at this hour, not managing his museum. I'd loved that place when I was little, especially when Mom and Dad couldn't get a sitter to watch me and they let me have the run of the exhibits. Growing up surrounded by old fossils and diaries made me realize that history had been people's real lives once. Someday my life was going to be some- body else's history. I found it fascinating, at least until I realized that most people from the past were just as boring and shitty as most people in the present.

Dad looked at me sideways, muting the TV. "You want to watch this?" he asked skeptically.

"It's wrestling," I said. I could take it or leave it.

Dad shrugged. He unmuted the TV, but I didn't feel welcome. I didn't know why. We'd watched WWE together before, although we seldom rooted for the same wrestler. He'd never acted like I was weird for wanting to watch it with him. I spent more time thinking about his reaction than watching the match. During the commercial break, it hit me.

Dad never thought it was weird before because he saw me as a guy before. I shaved and scratched myself and tucked myself up in my waistband to hide it when I got excited in public. Now I menstruated. Now I had cramps. I didn't know what Dad saw me as these days, but it wasn't his son.

"I got kicked off the soccer team today," I said, feeling him out.

Dad squared his jaw like he was angry. He was angry at me. "Yeah?"

I got up and went upstairs to my room. It felt safer there.

Dad was the one who'd decided I was a boy when I was born. But now, instead of defending my right to *stay* a boy, he'd withdrawn what little interest he used to take in me. It was like I'd let him down—or like I'd tricked him somehow. That was it, I suspected: he felt I'd made a fool of him. He would probably never forgive me for that.

Mom came home later and served us snow crab. Dad ate his alone in the living room, but she and I sat together in the dining room, beneath the chandelier. If I told her about what had happened to me in soccer today, she'd just start crying again, like everything was about her. Instead, I listened while she told me instead about her workday, how some little kid had said "ho ho ho" out of nowhere and made everybody on the tour laugh. Weren't little kids a riot? Mom's hair was pulled back in a ponytail, hands gesturing animatedly. She acted like nothing was different between us. If you pretended at something hard enough, maybe it became true.

"Mom?" I asked.

She looked up with a vague smile. "Hmm?"

"How do you get congenital adrenal hyperplasia?" I asked. "Like, how does it happen?"

Mom gave me a wide-eyed, distraught look. She scraped

the meat out of her crab leg. She took so long doing it that I thought she wouldn't answer me.

"CAH is recessive," Mom said. "Both the parents have to have a copy of the recessive gene."

"So you guys did this to me?" I asked.

Mom looked like I had struck her. Exasperated or not, I did feel guilty.

"I'm gonna go upstairs," I said, picking up my plate. "Finish my homework."

◆◆◆

This was a bad idea, I thought, standing before my closet mirror. With furry, taped-on muttonchops and fake fangs, I made for a respectable werewolf this Halloween. That was the problem, though. Halloween was so *dorky*. I consoled myself with the knowledge that Michelle was going to look dorky too. I didn't know what her costume would be—we liked to surprise each other every year—but there was no way to make Halloween look cool, period.

"Ashley!" Mom called out. "Door!"

I went downstairs to the foyer, but drew back. It wasn't Michelle. Corey was standing in the doorway, shuffling his feet, abashed. He was wearing a headband that made it look like someone had shoved a meat cleaver through his head—which you could believe of his mom, if you'd ever seen how much he liked to annoy her.

"I'm sorry, man," Corey rushed to say. "I know why you're pissed at me, and like, I'm sorry."

"Good," I said. "Get out."

"Ash, come on!" Corey begged. "We've been friends since we were nine."

"Yeah, I remember that," I said. "Did you remember when you were feeling me up?"

"I said I was sorry!" Corey whined. "I didn't mean it like that. I know it was wrong now. Mom said it was."

Now that I'd had time to cool my temper, I realized that I could either forgive him now or stay mad at him forever. Pulling dumb shit was what he did. I might as well resent spiders for sneaking into my bedroom to escape the cold outside.

"Okay," I said reluctantly. "Truce."

Corey punched me in the shoulder with a sigh of relief.

Michelle turned up not long later, and she was dressed as—wait for it—the tooth fairy. I'm serious; she was wearing a blue tutu with a string of bloody teeth for a belt. In a weird way, it was really cute. She bopped me on the head with her magic wand. The three of us were ready, so I said goodbye to Mom, and we left.

Salem Common was downtown, a wide-open park with benches and gazebos. Most of the time, there wasn't a whole lot going on there. Halloween was its one day to shine. The glow of the lampposts was like dancing flames on the pear-colored autumn trees, trunks wrapped with fairy lights. Tourists packed the paths so tightly it was hard to find space to walk. Partway down the main road, a local band made up of four women—all dressed like witches—were playing wailing violins. Somebody dressed like an orange *T. rex* chased a toddler onto the lawn. Farther out on the common, where the sidewalks intersected the park, police were busy erecting rental fences. I watched one guy chug a beer, then vomit it back up on his shoe.

Michelle and Corey and I leaned against a fence, the metal cold under our arms. A fire truck with angry red lights led the cavalcade, followed by Little Miss Salem, sitting and waving in the back of a convertible. Next came the mayor and his family on foot. Honestly, it was all pretty pointless. Why did people come all this way to watch these people walk from one end of the street to the other? What was so special about them? Just because this guy was the mayor didn't mean he didn't get morning wood and bad breath like the rest of us did.

The more the night went on, the rowdier the crowd grew. Fire-eaters dominated the asphalt. Somebody—probably a tourist—howled at the moon, like an idiot. Michelle and Corey and I walked away from the fence to buy doughnuts. Corey spotted one of his millions of cousins and ran off to chase him, but Michelle and I sat eating on a park bench next to a cauldron filled with dry ice. And we wondered why we were so cold.

"Hey, Ash?" Michelle asked. She ate like a bird, taking little nibbles all around her doughnut until it gradually grew smaller and slimmer.

I made a sound to let her know I was listening.

"I had a twin sister," Michelle said. "Before I was born."

I put my doughnut down on my lap. This was the first I'd heard of anything like this.

"Mom had really bad preeclampsia," Michelle said. "That's something that makes your blood pressure spike when you're pregnant. Nobody knows why certain women get it. Sometimes it can kill the mom and the baby. Or, well, babies, in our case. It interfered with my twin's growth, and the doctor said if my mom wanted to carry to term, she'd have to abort my twin."

"That had to have messed with her," I said.

"I'm sure it did," Michelle said. "I think it messes with me too, sometimes, Ash. Because it was totally random chance that my twin's fetus was compromised and mine was fine. It could've gone the other way, and then I wouldn't be here. I think about that a lot. This other person could be sitting here right now instead of me. Maybe she'd be real different from me. I don't know if she'd even be friends with you. I know I didn't deserve to live more than she did. But the same goes the other way."

"She'd *have* to be real different from you, Michelle," I said. "No one's like you."

Michelle smiled with her eyes downcast. I couldn't tell if she was happy or sad, though they weren't mutually exclusive.

"How come you told me this?" I asked. "Not that I mind."

"Well," said Michelle, shifting toward me in conspiracy. "I figure now we both know something important about each other that we didn't before. So we're even."

"Yeah?" I asked, raising my eyebrows. "We're even?"

"Well, I don't know," she said with a big, toothy grin. "But I like feeling as if we're in a secret club of two. We could call it . . . the Contemporary Witches of Salem. What do you think?"

What did I think? I'd never been so eager to join any club.

It was unbelievable how euphoric I felt. If you'd dared me to walk on air at that moment, I probably could have done it. It didn't matter what my body was doing these days, because I belonged to something. I belonged to her. I belonged.

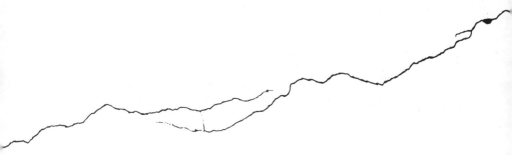

7

Once the reality of my having been kicked off the soccer team settled in, I fell into a major depressive spell. After all, I'd been obsessed with the sport since I was ten years old. One time, when I was twelve, I went around trying to convince my classmates to call it football, because that was what they did in the rest of the world.

If I'd been a lousy player, I think I would have cut my losses and looked for something else to do. But I was *good* at soccer. There was a reason I played striker on the team. For Coach to throw that away just because some parents were complaining . . . I didn't know what to call it except for a kick in the teeth.

I couldn't believe my actual skills mattered less than my junk, which shouldn't have been anybody's business but my own. And now that the period problem, as I'd dubbed it, was taken care of, it was like I was a regular guy again. My body couldn't possibly change on me in any other way.

I found out I was wrong one afternoon when I was doing nothing more offensive than walking to chemistry class. Eyes and snickers followed me down the hall. I'd gotten used to them—and what was I supposed to do, make a big stink every time? Then I noticed that every pair of intrusive eyes was aimed at my chest. I looked down but didn't see anything. No ketchup stains from lunch. No weird wrinkles from the wash.

In chemistry class, Ms. Fuller paired us up at the black-topped tables and gave us each a Bunsen burner. We were going to identify the different types of flame by color. I'd been paired with Matthew Sommerheim, whose mop of sandy hair and bangs had gone out of style a decade ago. Ms. Fuller turned her back on us, and his mouth snarled in a sort of sneer.

"Nice tits, Bishop," he said.

I asked to use the restroom. Mocking laughter followed me out the door, stinging my ears. The last thing I heard was the teacher shushing everybody, asking what had gotten into them. I bolted down the hallway to the men's room and swung the door open. When I looked in the mirror, I didn't see anything amiss. I zeroed in on my chest, and it took a while for me to realize what it was that others were seeing. My nipples were standing out. They'd never done that before. I lifted my shirt to just under my chin. The area around my nipples looked puffy. What the hell was going on?

Trying not to freak out, I took some Band-Aids out of my book bag and taped them over my nipples. When I pulled my shirt down, I couldn't see anything anymore. I turned at different angles just to be sure. The tape itched and pulled under my shirt. If I turned too quickly, it stung sharply. The back of my throat burned with panic. All I wanted was for this to *stop*.

I didn't see Michelle until lunch, and she knew something was wrong right away; she didn't just purse her lips, she wrinkled her forehead too. At our table, I told her what had happened, and her face went grim.

"I have a sports bra you can borrow," Michelle whispered.

"No," I said, a knee-jerk reaction. This couldn't be happening.

"Nobody has to know," Michelle said. "I'll go to my locker

and get it. Then I'll slip it to you under the table. You can return it when you have your own."

My own? My own bra? In what universe was I going to get my own bra? Guys didn't have tits, for Christ's sake!

When I went home at the end of the day, I shut myself up in my bedroom. The first thing I did was pull my shirt off and toss the bra to the floor in anger. I was trying to figure out my next move when Mom opened my door without knocking.

"Mom!" I yelled.

Mom's eyes fell on the bra, like they were specifically fine-tuned. And it hit me: this was the moment things were going to change for real between us. Until then, I was just her son who was going through some strange body changes. Now I was something else entirely: someone she could shape to her liking.

"Oh," Mom whispered. "We'll get you your own."

"Mom, no," I begged, mortified. "Please, I don't need a bra. I've got it covered."

"But you have to return that one, don't you?"

"But—"

"It's going to be fine, sweetie," Mom said.

I felt my heart sinking, my resolve crumbling. "But I don't want . . ."

"What if they grow bigger?" Mom pointed out. "Your breasts?"

One of my favorite words of old suddenly sounded dirty and foul. I tried picturing myself with them, large and unmistakable, and panicked.

"Make it stop," I said, my voice trailing off. "There's got to be some way. Make it stop."

"It's going to be okay," Mom said—like if she kept repeating it, she could wish it into reality.

She loaded me up in her car. In silence, we drove out to the Witch City Mall on Church Street. Its real name was Museum Place, but everyone called it Witch City so often that the nickname had overtaken the official one. It sounded spooky, but it was a regular shopping mall, the only difference being that it was one story, not two. The interior was depressing. I didn't know what it was about that place, but the moment you walked in, you got a desolate feeling. The restrooms were frequently out of order, too, with big lines stretching across from one store to another.

Mom took me to a ladies' underwear store, making me gag. Thankfully it was empty, because I didn't know what I would have done if I'd run into anyone from school. She grabbed a bunch of AA-cup bras out of the juvenile department.

"I never got to do this with Evie," Mom said. "She was so independent. Maybe that's why she moved to Boston."

I seized the first opportunity to stop talking about my chest. "She moved to Boston because she was tired of you talking crap about her girlfriend, Mom."

Mom fished in her purse for her wallet. "Evie doesn't know for sure that she's gay," she said quietly, no doubt afraid to be overheard. "She hasn't even tried being with a man."

"Okay," I said, "then how do you know that you're straight? You've never tried being with a woman."

Ordinarily I would have gotten into major trouble for a comment like that. But Mom was so busy envisioning the future with this new child of hers, I might as well have been a wall, or a dress-up doll. Nothing I said to her that evening sank in. She didn't care that I didn't want any of this. She only cared that it was happening, whether I wanted it or not.

Later that night, when I was alone in my room again, I shoved the new bras in my bottom drawer along with

Michelle's. I didn't want anything to do with them. I never wanted to see them again.

But I knew I was going to need one of them tomorrow, or school was going to be unbearable.

◆◆◆

If Halloween was the biggest holiday in Salem, Thanksgiving was probably a close second. It had something to do with romanticizing colonialism, I guess—but even if the first Thanksgiving happened the way people pictured it, it definitely didn't happen in Salem. Still, that didn't ward off all the cornucopias that went up on front doors as early as the start of November.

Thanksgiving felt kind of lonely in my house now that Evie had gone. Mom and Dad had stopped talking to her three years ago when she came home from college with a girlfriend, a perfectly nice girl who worked as a hairdresser. After the huge argument, Evie said she didn't understand why they were reacting that way. She said they had to have had some inkling about her, and I thought she was right. Not to stereotype, but a stranger could probably take one look at Evie and guess she was into girls. It was weird, I thought, that I was the one who was abnormal, and you couldn't tell it just by looking at me. Not in the past, anyway.

Normally Mom left ten dollars on my nightstand at the beginning of each month so I could go get my hair trimmed. But in November, I noticed she'd stopped doing it. At first I thought she'd forgotten. That was fine, but Thanksgiving rolled around, and she still hadn't given me any money. My hair was starting to look scruffy and untamed around my ears. I couldn't dip into my allowance for haircuts; I had to buy lunch at school, and now I had a birth control prescription to keep up with too. It wasn't that big of a deal, I told myself. If I skipped a haircut or two, I would still look better than Corey with his self-inflicted trims.

Thanksgiving without Evie tended to feel lonely, but that wasn't to say that the house was empty. Around four o'clock, all our relatives started showing up. Mom had three siblings—two brothers and a sister—who came back to Salem for this one occasion every year. Each one was louder than the last, making meek little Mom the odd one out.

By contrast, Dad's two brothers were grim and gruff. They didn't take their hats off even at the dinner table. Dad's mom was tiny, shriveled, and squinty, with a concentrated meanness about her jowls and eyes. She was the type of person who would camp outside Planned Parenthood, protesting with a *BABY MURDERERS!* sign on her lap. She was annoying for other reasons; for instance, she insisted on keeping her pet cat on her lap even at the table—and this was a mean little thing, just like its owner, scratching you if you tried to pet it.

There was nothing appetizing about turkey dinner. I didn't understand why it was the annual dish of choice when it tasted like chicken's inferior cousin. I finished my plate quickly, just so Mom wouldn't ply me with seconds, and went to the living room to hang out with my cousins—a freckle-faced girl in braces, two years younger than me, and a ten-year-old boy we thought might be autistic. Mostly we just sat playing on our phones, not talking to one another. Could you blame me? I didn't want to spend my time with a bunch of little kids, but it was better than spending time with their parents. I finally went upstairs to my room, where I got a text from Michelle.

mom burned the turkey (yay)! we ordered pizza

I felt myself smiling even before I sat down on my bed. **pizza and mac and cheese?** I asked, knowing all about her family's side dishes.

don't diss it until you've tried it, Michelle replied, along with the 100 emoji. **want to play salem online?**

Years ago, a local video game dev created this low-specs MMO called *Salem Online*. You played it with a dozen other people, friends or strangers, and your job was to figure out which of the players were witches and execute them. If you were playing as a witch, obviously your goal was to outsmart everyone and live until the end of the game. It was a pretty fun game, more strategy-based than something like *Minecraft*.

Logging into *Salem Online* on my phone, I saw that Michelle was already playing. We joined a party together and queued up with a couple of other familiar names; I thought I saw Corey's brother Curt, but I didn't have him on my friends list, so I wasn't sure. Once the game started, I didn't know which player Michelle was. The game worked like that, anonymizing everybody's names so people couldn't identify you. I squinted at the little figures on the screen anyway.

My role card told me I was playing as a witch. Awesome. In the private witches' chat, I tried feeling Michelle out, but she didn't respond when I said her name. She must not be playing as a witch with us. That seriously blew. It meant we were enemies this round.

In the public game chat, I switched strategies. I typed: **michelle sucks**

definitely, said one of the little gray-haired Puritan avatars.

Now that I knew which player she was, I cast a spell on her and turned her to stone. Unfortunately for me, she was playing as a minister, which meant she could communicate with her teammates while dead. The second I'd killed her, she blew my cover. The good guys voted me up to the gallows and hanged me.

Even without me, my team pulled through to victory. There had been plenty of times when Michelle won and I didn't, so I didn't feel too guilty about lording it over her. I called her to rub it in.

"You know, you're the worst," Michelle said. "You're the opposite of a sore loser. You're a sore winner."

"That doesn't sound right, somehow," I said.

"Hey, we should go to that new escape room downtown!" Michelle said. "It looks like fun. And we'd be guaranteed to be allies then, so you wouldn't get to be a jerk to me."

"Not sure I wanna be locked in a small room with you for an hour, nerd."

She blew raspberries through the phone.

"I'd better go," I said. "There might be some dessert left. I wanna grab it before it disappears."

"Okay," Michelle said. "Love you."

She hung up, leaving me holding my phone, staring at the blank screen. It meant nothing, I told myself. Michelle was a very affectionate person. She was always telling her friends she loved them, or sneaking up on them from behind, surprising them with a hug. It meant nothing if I thought her small body felt good against my back when she gave me one. I thought about the tiny green spot in the corner of her right eye, floating in a sea of brown.

It meant nothing.

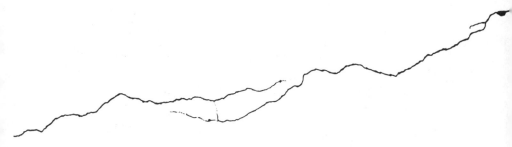

8

The week before winter break there was a scheduled school assembly. The entire student body packed into the uncomfortable wooden seats facing the auditorium stage. Purple was a weird choice of color for curtains, but it wasn't like I belonged to the drama club.

Principal Androse stood behind the lectern. His important announcement: Deodat Lawson High School was offering logic classes as an elective after winter break. Wasn't that exciting? I nodded off in my seat. When I woke up, bleary-eyed and bored, I had to go to the bathroom.

Leaving for the restroom was okay during assembly. In fact, a couple of students had already done it, though they probably weren't relieving themselves so much as they were gossiping by the sinks. I got out of my seat and left the auditorium. Before I could step into the restroom, my homeroom teacher, Mr. Proctor, came out through the door. We almost banged into each other. Mr. Proctor smoothed his hand over what little remained of his mousy, red-brown hair. He was such a tall guy, I wondered if his parents had fed him Miracle-Gro as a kid.

"Hey, Ash," Mr. Proctor said in his best "I'm a cool kid, just like you" voice. "Can I have a second? We've been talking about the bathroom situation."

What bathroom situation? Who were "we"?

"We think it might be more appropriate if you use the staff bathroom, just for a while," Mr. Proctor said. "Leaving you alone with all the boys . . . you can see how it might lead to harassment, discomfort—"

"I'm a guy." A guy who was getting tired of repeatedly having this discussion.

"I know, I know," Mr. Proctor said. "Nobody's arguing that. It's just that we want to do everything possible to prevent a hostile environment."

A hostile environment? Did he mean like a fight? Because if he meant a fight, I could easily hold my own.

"All right, Ash?" Mr. Proctor asked. "You can use our room and, if it's full, there's always the girls' room. You know how girls are—no one will bother you in there."

"If I were transgender," I said, "you'd let me use the guys' room." He'd have to. It was the law in Massachusetts.

"We discussed that," Mr. Proctor said. Again, who were "we"? "And, well—you're not transgender. It's different."

"Yeah, it's different because I'm not fucking transitioning," I said, having reached my breaking point. "I've always been a guy!"

Mr. Proctor raised his eyebrows. "Your condition was never disclosed to us when you enrolled here. That's a point of contention, actually, but given the circumstances, we're trying to be sensitive about this. And I'd rethink using that kind of language with faculty. I'm only not giving you detention because I understand where you're coming from— "

"If you understood where I was coming from, you'd leave me alone!"

"Ashley, lower your voice."

"Don't call me Ashley!"

He said he understood where I was coming from. He said that he sympathized. But if he had, he wouldn't have suspended me, which was exactly what he did—for "talking back to the faculty," which was a bogus charge if I'd ever heard one. I had to walk home before I could take a piss. When I emerged from the bathroom, seething with anger, I found out the school had already called Dad.

"You got suspended?" he roared at me.

He was standing in the little hallway in front of the bathroom. He swung his heavy fist at me. Reflexes helped me duck underneath it. I ran through the dining room and into the kitchen, but he followed me in, yelling. "On top of everything else, you got yourself fucking suspended?"

"It was the teacher's fault," I said, backing against the sink. "He was treating me like it didn't matter what I thought!"

"It *doesn't* matter what you think!"

Did he realize what he'd said? Did he stop to think what it felt like to be told that?

He breathed in and out through his squared jaw, like an angry bull. All his energy seemed to go toward glowering at me.

I went around the giant roadblock his body made, dodging when he swung halfheartedly at my shoulder. Upstairs, I lay on my bed and stared at the ceiling. I realized I was shaking.

Mom came home around seven o'clock. I heard it when she shut the door downstairs, when the steps creaked as she climbed them to the second floor. She opened my door and peeked inside. I was pretty sure I hadn't moved since lying down.

"Your dad just told me what happened," Mom said.

"It's not fair, Mom." My voice broke with emotion. I hated that.

Mom stepped into the room. "You really shouldn't curse at your teachers, Ashley."

"Why shouldn't I? He told me I have to use the girls' room."

"Would that be so bad?" Mom asked anxiously. "It's just a bathroom. You'd have privacy in the stalls."

I sat up against the headboard, staring at her, trying to understand her. She was wearing a wide-eyed, encouraging smile, but it wasn't working.

"Mom," I blurted out, "you know I'm still a guy, don't you?"

Mom faltered. She didn't know. I could have burst out crying right there and then.

"Mom!"

"Would it be so hard?" Mom asked. "Just trying it for a little while?"

How did you go about trying to be a girl? What did that even mean? In grade school, I'd belonged to the Cub Scouts. Some said that was a club for boys, but there had been plenty of girls in my troop, girls who liked hiking and camping and fishing along with the rest of us. Did that mean whenever they were with the Scouts, they weren't being girls? What were they supposed to do instead, knit and bake? I didn't know, or care to know, how to knit. I didn't know how to bake, except for this one recipe I prepared very rarely, sweet potato muffins. You know where I learned how to make them? In Cub Scouts. Was I being a girl when I made them? Were there moments in time when we stopped being who we were, just because we didn't follow expectations?

What the hell was everyone expecting of me?

"Just try it," Mom urged. "Things might get easier if you do."

Well, it would have to wait until after Christmas. I'd been suspended for a whole week.

◆◆◆

49

Just because I had the week off from school didn't mean I was allowed to shirk my studies. My teachers emailed me assignments at the end of every day and expected them back the following morning. Dad must have thought they weren't punishing me hard enough; he gave me extra chores around the house. I changed the tires on his car, put chains on them, and cleaned the snowy birds' nests out of the gutter. I was supposed to try being a girl now, but when it came to traditionally masculine chores, Dad seemed to have no qualms about foisting them all on me.

That Monday was the last day of school for my classmates. Corey texted me to say he was going to California with his parents; he wouldn't be back until after New Year's. He was the only one of my guy friends who still spoke to me, but he didn't ask to hang out anymore. It was lonely. Sometimes I reread old texts just to pretend I still had friends.

I still had Michelle, though. Michelle's parents never left town for Christmas, though she had an uncle from Boston who sometimes spent the holiday with them. She came to visit me on Monday, bundled up in a scarf and earmuffs. She stamped her feet on the throw rug inside the front door, shaking the snow off her shoes. It was still coming down outside, light and powdery.

"Merry Christmas!" Michelle said. "Brought you your present early."

She handed me a square package covered in lumpy silver wrapping paper. I let her inside and heaved the door shut.

"Jeez," I said. "Why not tomorrow? Got somewhere better to be?"

"Church," Michelle said. "They're going to try and save my heathen soul."

"Brave of them."

I took her to my bedroom, where I had a present for her

too. I wasn't any good at gift wrapping. I'd folded it up and stuffed it in an old shoebox.

"Okay," Michelle said, plopping down on my bed with her gift on her lap. "You open yours first."

I tore off the paper. Inside was a book, which most people wouldn't have thought to get me. It was a biography of Adrian Doherty, who was possibly the greatest soccer player England had ever seen—better than Beckham, than Giggs, than Neville and Scholes. A bunch of unlucky injuries cut his career short before he could ever play for Manchester United. It was the story of a flame that flickered out too early.

I knew Michelle wasn't making any kind of statement with the gift. Probably she'd heard me mention Doherty before and knew I was interested in him. Now, with my condition dogging me at every step, I wondered if I'd turn out like him. I could have been somebody. I was a great soccer player. I never missed a single practice. None of that mattered once people found out my body wasn't shaped exactly like theirs.

"Thanks," I said. "It looks awesome."

"I'm so glad," Michelle said. "You're hard to shop for, you know?"

"How am I hard to shop for? You could've just bought me pork rinds."

"You eat those the rest of the year. It wouldn't have been special."

"Open yours, nerd."

She took the lid off the shoebox and pulled out the black, oversized T-shirt. It was the one I'd had signed by the members of the Skeletronics, the time Mom took Corey and me to see them in Melrose.

Michelle's eyes widened. She held the shirt up in both hands. "Why are you giving this to me?"

I shrugged. "You like the Skeletronics more than I do."

She knew it wasn't true. We were pretty equally fanatical about them. But the Skeletronics were never coming to Salem—few bands did—and, I don't know . . . giving her something with that much personal meaning made it more special, I thought.

She seemed to understand. She lowered the shirt to look at me soberly. I was still standing; it felt like there was a huge, unbearable distance between us. I was afraid to come closer.

"You really like me," Michelle said quietly. "Don't you?"

That was something else that scared me. Had I been too obvious?

I was saved from having to answer when Mom called me downstairs to help her hang garlands on the fireplace. Michelle decided she had better go home. She hopped off the bed—she was so petite, her feet hadn't touched the floor when she was up there—and slipped out the door. Her hair gleamed around her ears in a puffy brown cloud. I was so screwed.

❧❧❧

Michelle's wasn't the only family going to church on Christmas Eve. She went to the predominantly Black church in Lynn, about a fifteen-minute drive away. My family's church was on Essex Street, which meant we had to walk there. It was called First Church, and it literally was the first church in Salem. In the old days, I'm sure it was all fire and brimstone with the Puritans running things. Now the clergy were much friendlier, promoting a message of unity and belonging.

Mom and Dad and I trudged out there in our snow boots. I'd never liked the cold, and I was feeling miserable in my thick blue coat, my face chapped raw by the wind.

The exterior of the building looked ancient to the untrained eye. Actually, it had been renovated in the mid-1800s, so it was anybody's guess what it had looked like before then. The English Gothic stone roof had parapets on it, like the Puritans had anticipated being attacked by somebody. On the outside, the church looked like it comprised multiple towers. But once we went in through the red doors, the inside was so small that I'd always figured the extra towers must be hiding something—maybe old witch-torturing devices, or the *Malleus Maleficarum* itself.

The walls around us were cream-colored with pastel stained glass windows. The red pews were done up in a peculiar style, the backs of them stiff and straight, not slanting like you usually saw in a church. Most were filled already, parishioners wearing their stockings and smart suits. A colonial American flag stuck out of the flagpole bracket to the left of the altar, mirrored by the state flag to its right. As for the ceiling, the shiny black lattices made me feel like I was looking through bars on a window at a cloud of snow on the other side.

Christmas was ostensibly about God, but the only time God seemed relevant was in church. What did I believe about God? Even now I wasn't sure. Jesus was probably a real person. Contemporary historians had mentioned him in their writings, though they seemed to think of him as a rabble-rouser at best. It wasn't until a century or so later that his follower count swelled. I guess we would call that going viral today.

A lot could get distorted in a century's time. Did this guy really raise the dead? Maybe he was a particularly good physician, and Lazarus was only in a coma. Did he fake his death on the cross? Maybe he took something to slow his blood and put him in a deep sleep. Maybe I was an unbeliever and I was going to hell. I'll say this, though. If the historical Jesus was anything like the biblical one, loving everyone unconditionally—even the ones who condemned him to die—I didn't see how he could have it in his heart to send anybody to hell. What I could see was why people would single him out and murder him. He was too different. Too freakish.

God might be real or might be fake; I didn't know. I felt like my existence was evidence against his. My body was the result of an accident in the womb. I was literally a freak mutation, not at all evidence of a perfect, intelligent designer with his hand in every person's life. If God were real, and if God were kind, he wouldn't have been cruel or thoughtless enough to make me.

♦♦♦

On Christmas morning, I padded out of bed and into the corridor outside my room. I sat in the cushioned window seat, gazing out at our backyard. It wasn't much to look at: a small storage shed, a utility pole whose purpose mystified all of us, and a low fence where vines twined around the chain links in summer. The whole backyard was quilted in thick snow. It looked like someone had poured white milk all over the concrete, then stood back and watched it freeze over. The cold reached through the window, fogging it up. I wiped a circle on it to see better, the soft side of my fist coming away wet. A liminal time like this made me believe in rebirth.

Still in pajamas, I went downstairs. The Christmas tree in the living room sparkled in gold garland and twinkling fairy lights, the house so quiet I could hear the filaments snapping in the bulbs. A red velvet cloth served as the tree skirt, the thirsty trunk sucking up the water in the bucket.

"Merry Christmas," Mom said. She came up behind me, palming my head.

All the gifts under the tree made it look like we'd gone nuts this year, but I knew the bulk of them came from relatives and family friends. I'd bought Dad a new pipe, Mom a Christmas cactus; she liked gardening. Dad was still asleep, and we both knew better than to wake him. Mom and I opened our gifts in companionable silence, torn wrapping paper littering the carpet like scraps of confetti. Mom had bought me a lamp shaped like a soccer ball, which I thought was pretty funny. Laughing, I asked if I could go upstairs and plug it in.

"Wait," Mom said. She handed me a gift bag.

I pulled out the tissue paper and looked inside. There had to be some kind of mistake. I pulled out a plastic bag filled with different shades of lipstick, mascara, and eyebrow pencil.

"Is this a joke?" I asked. My throat felt dry and cold.

"I just thought," Mom began, "since you're going to try . . ."

"Why would you do this today?" I asked, choking. "Did you really think I would like this?"

"You don't have to use it right away," Mom said. "I could help you—"

"I'm not going to school with lipstick on!"

"Ashley . . ."

"I'm going upstairs," I said, collecting the wrapping paper on the floor. "I don't feel good."

"Ashley, please," Mom said tightly, eyes misting over. "It's Christmas."

I hated this. I hated when she acted like she was about to cry, because it made me feel like the worst person on the planet. I didn't know if she knew she was doing it. I knew it was selfish of her.

You will keep silent, Bridget Bishop said all those years ago. I held my tongue. I bit it, actually, until I tasted blood, in the interest of keeping the peace.

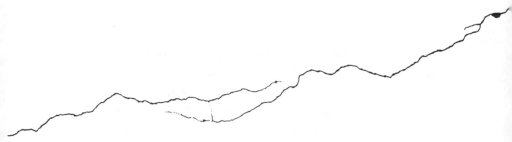

9

"The travelers had now reached the verge of the wooded country," Miss Dawson read in a hushed, excited tone. She paced up and down between our desks, carrying her copy of *Ivanhoe* as though it were a part of her hands. "Notwithstanding the lateness of the hour, Cedric and Athelstane counted themselves secure . . ."

I crossed my legs under my desk, pressing my thighs together. I had to piss, and I still had two more classes after this. I chanced a look at the clock on the wall, willed the hands to move faster so that the end of the school day would come and I could race home to relieve myself.

"The outlaws, whom the severity of the forest laws had reduced to this roving, desperate mode of life . . ."

God, I wished she would shut up. It felt like she was slowing the clock down just by talking.

"They were surprised to find a horse litter placed upon the ground, beside which sat a young woman, richly dressed in the Jewish fashion."

Wow, that sounded vaguely racist.

The bell took mercy on me and finally rang. "Oh," Miss Dawson said, disappointed. "Already?" My classmates around me were climbing out of their seats. "Well," she said, "if you'd be so kind as to read the next chapter on your own time.

Tomorrow we'll be discussing warfare. How does *Ivanhoe* conflate warfare with the family unit?"

I couldn't take it anymore. I slung my bag over my shoulder and bolted out of the room. I raced to the end of the hall, around the corner, and down the next hall, where I tried the door on the staff bathroom.

Locked. Shit! What, did they only have one stall in there? I doubled back, frantic, and stopped outside of the girls' room. I looked with dread at the swinging, nondescript door.

My kidneys were bursting. I just couldn't take it anymore. I slipped inside.

Christ, it had these nauseatingly pink walls. What was the point of that? Where were the urinals? I supposed girls just used the toilet, like I did when I was at home. That led me to wondering how they got their business done without a penis. Did it come out of the same place the blood did? Or maybe they had another opening somewhere. A lot of stuff about girls mystified me, and slightly creeped me out, if I was being honest. And I was supposed to try being one. Yeah, good luck with that.

"Uh, what are you doing in here?"

I stopped with my hand on the door to a stall. Rachel Bloombury, a freshman, was standing by the sink with a girl I didn't know. Both of them were staring at me.

"Why are you in the girls' room?" Rachel asked, like I was out of my mind.

"Because I have to pee," I said. "That's generally the reason people use the bathroom."

"You can't be in here," said Rachel's horror-struck friend, who seemed even younger than Rachel did somehow. "You could perv on one of us!"

"Why would I perv on one of you?" I asked. "Hairless little kids don't do it for me."

"Hairless?"

"I'm gonna tell the principal you were in here," Rachel said, even as I disappeared inside the stall, swinging the door shut behind me. "You're gross!"

There was just no way to win, was there?

After I relieved myself, I went to history class, trying my best to push the incident from my mind.

After history, I had PE. I arrived early in the overheated gym with its windowless walls and shiny floors. Miss Martin wasn't there yet. In the hall outside, a girl had pulled her over to talk, claiming it was an emergency.

"There she is," Jay Tulley said.

He didn't mean Miss Martin; he was talking about me. He came at me with Evan Carmichael and Ryan St. Paul. A few girls leaned in the doorway, peering into the hall outside. I realized now that they were keeping a lookout.

"I'm going out with Louisa now," Jay told me.

"Good luck with that," I said, hiding how nervous I felt. What was taking the teacher so long?

"You know how disgusted she is, knowing you put your hands all over her?" Jay asked. "Knowing she had to kiss you?"

"She seemed pretty into it at the time," I said. Why couldn't I check my loud mouth at the door?

"She never wanted to date a dyke," Jay said. "So I told her I'd do this for her."

Ryan circled behind me, grabbing my arms. I slammed my shoulder back to knock him off. He stumbled away, but Evan was right there, grabbing me around the waist. Cowards. Did it make them feel strong, ganging up on me three to one? Did it feel good knowing they couldn't take me in a fair fight?

Jay punched me in the face. Stinging pain burst across my mouth. My lip collided with my teeth, breaking open, puffing up. He punched me in the stomach. It tightened and flexed all on its own, like it did when I was about to throw up. I prayed I wouldn't. I didn't think I could handle the embarrassment. He punched me in the dick and I was winded, buckling over, stars swimming in my watery eyes. I heard somebody yelling. I realized it was me.

"Miss Martin's coming!" a girl said.

The guys leaped off of me. They scattered to different sides of the gym like nothing had happened, the girls trailing after them, equal parts giggly and anxious. A small part of me was pleased to see Jay shaking out his fist, evidence that I had hurt him back.

Miss Martin stepped inside, her hair bobbing in a high ponytail. She looked down at me and frowned. I hadn't realized I was sitting on the floor. I licked the blood off my bottom lip.

"Ashley," she said. "No fighting during school hours."

I tried to tell her to go fuck herself, but I was so wheezy that I couldn't form the words. Breathing actually hurt. It was my pride that kept me from screaming in pain—although I'm sure the breathlessness helped too.

Miss Martin dismissed me from gym class early to see the school nurse. On my way there, a tooth fell out of my mouth. Frightened, all I could think to do was pick it back up and put it in my pocket. The nurse gave me some aspirin, then sent me home with instructions to lie down.

I was terrified at how mad Dad was going to be. I didn't even consider calling Mom for help. I sat down in the kitchen like a zombie for two hours until she came home. I must have looked worse than I thought, because she gasped when she saw me.

"Who hit you?" she cried.

"Just some guys at school," I said. I wasn't a snitch.

"Boys? Boys hit you?" she asked, her hands clasped together in front of her mouth, eyes shimmering already.

"Mom, stop." My voice came out with a slight lisp. I didn't know what had done it: the swelling, or the missing tooth.

"I'll call the dentist," Mom said, rushing to the wall phone. I could see her debating with herself internally before she pulled out her cell phone instead. Why was she so keen on never using the home phone? Sometimes I wondered if she was waiting for Evie to call. If she was, she was deluding herself.

I listened with one ear while Mom made an appointment for tomorrow afternoon. When she hung up, she stuffed her phone in her pocket, looking at me with obvious anguish.

"I can't believe boys hit you," she said. "What kind of parents do they have?"

"Mom," I said. "Guys have fights at school all the time."

"But they know you're a girl now," Mom said. "And they hit you anyway?"

I put my head on the table between my arms, tuning her out.

❧ ❧ ❧

On Friday, Mom took me to the dentist, and he installed something called a port in my gums. His drilling into my jawbone hurt worse than the beating had. He sent me home; I went back the next day for the implant, an artificial tooth that looked like the real thing. He said I'd have to spend two weeks eating soft food and soup. He said I was lucky it was just a premolar that had been knocked out, not a more important tooth, which would have taken months longer to heal. I sure didn't feel lucky. I was just an ingrate, I guess.

Dad didn't find out about the new tooth until Sunday. Just as I'd thought, he was furious.

"A thousand bucks for a new tooth? Are you kidding me?"

"Jim, a bunch of boys beat him up," Mom said tremulously. "We couldn't just let him go without. It'd look unprofessional once he grew up . . ."

"Once he grows up, it'll be his damn problem."

"But he'd—she'd be bullied."

I gritted my teeth. Mom didn't seem able to decide which pronouns to use for me. I'd heard her flip-flopping like this before, apparently changing her mind from sentence to sentence. Every time I heard her refer to me as "she" or "her," my stomach twisted.

"Who hasn't been bullied in school?"

"Now they're beating her up. You know it'll only get worse." Mom summoned her bravery and said, "She should go to private school, like I did."

"Private school? You think I'm made of money?"

Well, wasn't he? He was descended from old Salem blood; his ancestors had received reparations for the witch trials, and they'd continued to do well for themselves in the centuries since.

"I just think," Mom said delicately, "that all the problems he's having right now will go away in private school. It would be better. For all of us."

That was why Dad agreed, in the end. I was such a burden for him, after all. He must have wanted nothing more than for the burden to go away.

❧❧❧

On Wednesday morning, Mom drove me to Winter Street in East Salem. We lived on Summer Street, in West Salem, and if you tried to make a congruent map of the town, the two streets would have been perfect mirror images of one another. The illusion fell apart once you put the map down. Most of Winter Street's houses were no taller than one story, packed close together like sardines in a can. The siding had actual color to it, reds and blues and greens with planters in the windows. Now and again the odd mansion stuck out like a sore thumb. There were oak trees all along the sidewalk, which gave me the impression that in summer, Winter Street must be a cool and shadowy place. The snow had thawed now. The trees were still dead, leafless and barren with white marks on the gray trunks where some of them had weathered the trials of disease. It was quiet here in a way that Salem rarely was, a residential area with no connection to any of the town's more important hubs.

Toward the end of the street was a building I might have taken for another mansion: beige, three stories, kind of colonial-looking, standing on a raised porch with skinny supports like toothpicks. Double colonial flags flanked the staircase. The sign on the lawn said, *Samuel Parris Private Academy*. Painted across the gutter in yellow were the words, *NO PARKING AT ANY TIME.*

"I went to school here when I was your age," Mom said, leading me up the walkway. "I should have had you here all along. It's wonderful. I promise you'll like it."

Inside, a cool white hallway greeted us, with backless benches and hanging portraits of snooty men in powdered wigs. We sat on one of those benches until we were called into a room with a long, skinny desk. The woman sitting behind it was in her sixties. She looked like she had had plastic surgery at some point, because her forehead was smooth and free of wrinkles, but her eyes were pinched too high at the corners. Her chin-length hair was a shade of blond I didn't even know came in a bottle.

"Do my eyes deceive me?" she began warmly. "Nicole Burroughs?"

"Nicole Bishop now," Mom said, beaming.

The two of them talked like old friends, sharing memories of Mom's days as a schoolgirl. They occasionally paused to laugh or sigh. Finally it came time for them to talk about me.

"We usually don't allow middle-of-the-year transfers," said the principal, Mrs. Eaton. "But for the daughter of an alumna . . ."

"Ashley's a good student," Mom lied. "A little rough around the edges, but—"

"But that just means she's strong-willed, doesn't it?"

Why? Why? Why did they keep saying "she"? Every time they said it, it felt like a rusty knife in my gut. All I could do was wince around the discomfort.

They decided to take me on a tour of the school. We went to the basement, where there was an indoor pool; then the topmost floor, where there was an observatory. I followed them, but I felt like I was watching things from outside of my body, hovering somewhere by the ceiling. We ended the tour back at Mrs. Eaton's office. She handed me a winter uniform: solid red blazer, gray knee socks, checkered red skirt. I unfolded the garments, the material scratchy in my hands. I felt like I'd been handed a prison uniform.

"Oh," Mom gasped. "You're going to look so good in that."

"This is a dress," I said. The weight of it exhausted me.

Mrs. Eaton peered at me across her desk as though I were an insect under a glass. "We think it would be best if you wore the girls' uniform. It'll cause less confusion. For all of us," she stressed.

Maybe it caused less confusion for her. I didn't know. All I knew was that I didn't know anything. I didn't know why this was happening. I didn't know why everyone was okay with it but me.

When we got back in Mom's car, she said, "I think this is going to work out really well for you, honey. And once you're settled in, we can look at getting all your records updated—"

"My records?"

"Well, yes, your birth certificate and your license and . . ." She waved a hand vaguely. "Just to have everything consistent. Maybe over the summer, when we have the time."

Back at home, I tossed the uniform on my bed. I opened my closet door; and I was so startled by my reflection, I stared back at it. Where had this girl come from? Unruly dark hair reached nearly to her chin. Her chest swelled under the confines of her bra. My airways tightened; I couldn't swallow. What had she done to me? I couldn't see me anymore.

10

With my new school as far away as Winter Street, I couldn't just walk there, at least not when it was so cold out. Mom had to drive me, and somehow that was almost as embarrassing as having to wear a fucking dress. Almost.

Mrs. Eaton had given me a map of the school, along with a paper schedule. When Mom dropped me off for my first day, I followed the map to the end of the corridor, my schoolbag empty. I went in a classroom on my right and found the seats filled with quiet, well-behaved students. A few of them talked among themselves in low whispers, but there was none of the screaming or jostling I was accustomed to from public school. Without screaming, could you even say it was a high school?

The split second it took for me to stand in the doorway surveying my surroundings seemed to stretch on infinitely. Terror overwhelmed me when heads turned my way, two girls and one guy. What would they think when they saw a guy in a dress looking back at them? It was like that dream where you're standing naked in the middle of a crowd—and in my case, standing there naked would probably have had the same effect.

But they didn't do anything. They didn't see anything out of the ordinary. They looked back at the board, or down at their phones. Somehow that terrified me even more.

I took a seat by the window, the fucking dress making

my thighs cold. Maybe you wouldn't have called it a window, because there was more glass than wall. It overlooked an actual Zen garden, a bridge of rocks stretched across a trickling, human-made pond. I knew it was human-made because it hadn't frozen over; the pump circulating the water probably must be keeping it warm. The teacher walked in, carrying a coffee cup, and everybody but me sat up straight. She was a gray-haired woman, her square eyeglasses poorly fitted to her sheeplike face. Appropriately enough, she was wearing a woolen dress.

"Hello, everyone," she said in a soothing voice. "We have a new student. Everyone please be kind to Ashley Bishop."

A couple of students mumbled "Hello" or "Hi." It was hard to be enthusiastic this early in the morning. The teacher, whose name was Miss Marbury, turned and looked at me, smiling. Her underbite protruded from her lower lip. Had it been the top one, she could have been a rabbit, which made me feel conflicted about the details of her taxonomy.

"Ashley is descended from a prominent witch trial victim," Miss Marbury said. "Do you want to tell us about her, Ashley?"

Not really, I thought. "Bridget Bishop," I said, my elbow on my desk.

"Bridget Bishop was the first woman hanged in Salem on witchcraft accusations," Miss Marbury informed the rest of the class.

Great. Private school must do their annual witch trial lectures in winter instead of autumn.

"But actually," Miss Marbury said, "she wasn't the first Salemite executed for witchcraft—just the first one executed on land."

This was the first I'd heard of that. I lifted my head, partly paying attention.

"The first American victim of witch hysteria was named

Mary Lee," Miss Marbury said. A couple of my classmates moved to open their notebooks. "But she never even made it to American soil. She was en route when her ship ran into a terrible storm. The other Puritans on board thought that God must be angry with them. In order to appease him, the rest of the passengers tried and executed Mrs. Lee for witchcraft. To understand how something like this could happen, it's important to understand what the Puritans believed in.

"The Puritans followed the Bible closely, with one caveat. They believed that they, and not the Jews, were God's chosen people. Because of this covenant, they were the only people guaranteed to go to heaven when they died. All other humans were condemned to hell even before they had been born. Being God's chosen people, they couldn't reconcile it when misfortune fell upon them. Their answer to this contradiction was witchcraft.

"Witchcraft allowed Puritans to put the blame on outside forces whenever it seemed that God had done the impossible and turned his back on them. Any time blight befell a farm, or a town suffered a food shortage, someone would be singled out as a witch and killed. And if the disasters didn't stop with the witch's death, that meant there must have been more witches hiding in plain sight. You can see how such a climate would lead a sleepy little town to kill twenty of its own residents."

"What disaster happened in Salem?" I asked. I'd forgotten to raise my hand.

Miss Marbury smiled her almost-rabbit smile. "Likely it was ergotism," she said. "It's a disease you get when you eat moldy rye. It can cause seizures and hallucinations—just like little Ann Putnam and Abigail Williams experienced before all the accusations started. Rye was Salem's primary crop back then. And Salem was just coming out of the end of a miniature ice age, so all the rye was very damp. Perfect for growing mold."

I wanted to ask some more questions, but just then, the fire alarm started ringing. Everybody packed up their books and jumped out of their chairs.

"Fire drill," whispered the guy next to me, like I couldn't figure that out for myself. He was tall, lanky, and white as chalk, hair shaved close to his head in a buzz cut. He shot me a grin, and I raised my eyebrows and shrugged. I didn't feel ready to smile at anyone yet.

◆◆◆

I wasn't sure how much I liked my new school. When my classmates went to their lockers between classes to exchange books, there was none of the usual gossip, flirtations, girls swapping lipsticks and guys swapping memes. I kind of missed the liveliness—even if I didn't miss getting catcalled or mockingly asked to spare a tampon. I ought to have felt safe, I thought. But the strangest thing was that I didn't. Pretending I was a girl, I felt less safe than I ever had.

The cafeteria was full of these big round tables with rounded ergonomic benches. Against the back wall was an actual flatscreen TV playing what looked like *Finding Nemo*. That was great news if you were a six-year-old. I looked around for an empty table but couldn't seem to find one. A pretty Black girl with some space at her table spotted me and waved me over. She seemed friendly enough, so I carried my lunch to her table and sat down. She had a very tired face. Her box braids were so heavy that I could hear it when they knocked against one another.

"Welcome to Sam Parris," she said. She was too tired even to smile. "Did anyone welcome you? I'm Naia Caldwell, your class rep."

"Thanks," I said.

"We've got loads of extracurriculars. There's a chess club, a debate club, and a swim team. We're trying to get basketball and soccer added to the roster."

"Yeah?"

"What do you like best?"

"I played soccer at my old school."

"Was it a public school? I don't know of many private schools with a girls' soccer team."

The lanky guy from history class came over and sat down with us. "What's good, Naia?"

"Hey," Naia said. She kissed him. She still didn't smile.

"Hey," said the guy to me. He told me his name was Tyler.

"Hey," I said. We sounded like a flock of parrots.

"Did I hear you say you like soccer?" Tyler asked.

"She was on the team in her old school," Naia said, leaning against his shoulder.

"What position did you play?" Tyler asked.

"Forward," I said. I felt like I was answering for somebody else.

"Nice!" Tyler said. "I love soccer. Suck at it, though. Maybe the three of us can head down to Salem Common when it's warm again."

"I haven't played in three months," I warned. I was rusty as hell.

"Works out well for me," Tyler said.

"Why'd you stop playing that long ago?" Naia asked, tilting her head. "Were you injured?"

"Sort of," I said.

In a way, talking to these two was a nice change from being ostracized. Something about it still didn't feel right, though. If I had to become somebody else to be accepted, what good was that? Why wasn't I any good the way I already was?

Michelle thought I was good the way I was. She was the only person who felt that way these days. Maybe you didn't need a whole slew of people if you had the one who mattered most.

I'd texted Michelle only sporadically since Christmas. She'd sent me a message asking if I was all right after I stopped showing up at school, but I'd changed the topic. If just thinking about her made me feel better, being near her would probably make me feel exponentially better. But I was worried what she would think when she saw the girl who had taken my place.

"Ashley," Naia said, "you've got a faraway look on your face. You must be thinking about a boy."

Somehow I kept from puking all over her. First impressions were key.

♠ ♠ ♠

At the end of the day, I climbed in the front seat of Mom's car, settling my schoolbag between my feet.

"How was it?" Mom asked tentatively as I buckled in and she backed out of her parking space.

In the interest of keeping the peace, I shrugged. "It was fine. Just school."

She seemed to take this as verbal confirmation that the stars were in alignment and baby Jesus was smiling down on us. She chatted the whole way home about how much easier my life was going to be as a girl. Except I wasn't a girl, I thought, leaning against the window and tuning her out. I was just playing at being one so people would leave me the hell alone.

Mom dropped me off at home but had to leave again to go back to work. I went upstairs to my room to put a dent in my homework. Unsurprisingly, I didn't make much progress. I took out my phone and texted Michelle.

still want to go to an escape room? I asked.

I was worried she'd leave me on read. But a few minutes later she replied.

where have you been?

switched schools, I typed, though by now that was self-evident. **some guys beat me up. had to.**

yeah, i know they beat you up, ash. It was just a text, but I could tell how worried she was—and, I gathered, a little hurt. **why haven't you kept up with me? did you think i would side with them?**

She might have, if she knew the way I was thinking about her lately. I didn't say that. **i just didn't want to talk to anyone. i'm sorry.**

There was a pause. Then she said, **it's ok. i can't imagine how i'd feel right now if i were you.**

That was another reason Michelle was so great. We almost always saw eye to eye, and when we didn't, our disagreements didn't last long.

so, Michelle said. **you want to try the new escape room?**

not so new anymore, I typed.

that's your fault. :p

least we avoided the holiday rush.

go on saturday?

sounds great.

When we were done texting, I absentmindedly pulled up my Skeletronics playlist. I set it to shuffle. A song called "From the Ashes" started playing. I'd always gotten a kick out of that song, mostly because I shared a name with it. It was about a robot waking up under a gallows tree, like the one from which my famous ancestor had been hanged. For a split second, I had in my mind's eye an image of myself hanging from that tree. The next second, it was gone.

I decided I needed some food to get my brain back on track.

◆◆◆

Michelle lived on North Street, which—get ready for a shocker—was the street directly north of mine. The name made sense if the people who coined it first came from Summer Street, but considering it was nowhere near North Salem, the name gave tourists a low opinion of Salemites. I considered that impression accurate, though for unrelated reasons.

The houses on North Street were pretty glamorous, but a few had been neglected over the years, the cost of the upkeep too much for families whose prosperous ancestors blew their cash on booze and slaveholding. Michelle's house was somewhere in the middle. It had a blue-gray exterior, and there were bicycles and rubber balls lying on the dead grass in the front yard. Michelle had two younger brothers, both menaces. I'd met them a couple of times and probably aged four years from each experience. Sometimes I was glad I had no younger siblings of my own.

When I knocked on the door, Michelle's dad distractedly let me inside. The front hall was hardwood, narrow but very long, with a multitude of doors on either side of it; it made me feel like I was walking between compartments on a train. I went past the grandfather clock at the end of the hall and went upstairs to Michelle's bedroom, taking off my coat as I went. I was accustomed to just letting myself in—if she'd been changing or something, she would have locked the door—so I did that.

Michelle's walls were turquoise, her favorite color. There were fairy lights above her headboard, Pokémon plush toys sitting on her bed. Weeb. The Skeletronics shirt I'd given her was hanging on her closet door. She was sitting on the plush rug, stuffing some books in her book bag, when she saw me. She gasped so loudly at the sight of me that I flinched.

"What . . . what happened to you?" Michelle asked.

It was the question I'd been waiting for, but I didn't have an answer. "Mom told me to try it," I recited dully.

Michelle's eyes watered. She pressed her fist to her mouth. She looked like she had just watched me die or something.

"You're not happy," she said, almost accusingly.

Could that really be the worst part of all this? I shrugged. "Ash . . ."

"I'm hanging out with you," I said. "I'm okay right now."

She didn't seem convinced. In fact, I had to get her to drink some tea to calm down before we left the house. I wished we could have taken Lynde Street downtown, but the bus route there was one-way. We were going to have to hoof it to Hawthorne Boulevard.

Neither of us said much as we walked. *Just be normal*, I kept thinking, though I wasn't sure if the thought was directed more at her or at myself. *Please let this just be a normal, chill, fun afternoon. Let me just be Ash again for a little while.* The trees on Essex Street were all dead, providing an unobscured view of the novelty shops: the oldest witchcraft store in America; the clothing boutique Michelle frequented; and the tourist-trap gift shops selling souvenirs. At the end of the street was Hawthorne Boulevard, where we boarded the bus. I didn't know about Michelle, but my feet were freezing in my shoes by then. We sat hunched over her phone, watching random videos to pass the time.

We got off the bus on Brown Street, not far from my new school. On Washington Square North, we went to a building that looked like a warehouse, at least on the outside. Apart from the receptionist's desk, which was starkly normal-looking, the lobby was a bizarre tribute to ancient Egypt. The walls were yellow, and there were cat statues everywhere. We paid the fare and got shown into the main room with twelve other people.

The door clicked shut behind us as the lights dimmed. The floor was dusted with real sand. The walls looked paved from dark bronze blocks, inscribed with hieroglyphs. A sarcophagus lay on the floor with a statue of Horus, the falcon-headed god, overlooking it. The only other decorations were some standing torches and shelves.

And, of course, the clock. Glowing near the ceiling, its red digits began the twenty-minute countdown. A disembodied voice told us this tomb housed a vengeful pharaoh's spirit. If we didn't get out of here in time, he would rise from the dead and slaughter us all.

"How?" I asked. "We outnumber his decrepit corpse fourteen to one."

"Don't ruin it," Michelle said.

We were looking for a hidden key that we were supposed to insert in the sarcophagus to keep it from opening up. My first thought was that it was buried in the sand, but searching for it there accomplished nothing except making my hands and jeans dirty. It was somebody else who suggested that the hieroglyphs might contain clues. I listened with one ear while the group gathered around and discussed the best way to decode them.

"Look," said one guy. "It's obviously telling us to blow out the torches."

"Blow them out? Not light them?"

"They're already lit . . ."

We blew them out and waited for the wax to cool. Sure enough, there was an ankh-shaped key swimming in the bottom of one of the torch bowls. I stood back and listened as every-body raced to lock the sarcophagus in the dark. We solved the puzzle with nine minutes to spare. It was kind of disappointing. I'd wanted to see what would happen if the timer ran out.

When Michelle and I went back to the lobby, I even asked the receptionist.

"There's a guy sitting in the sarcophagus," she said. "If time runs out, he jumps out at you."

"Wow," I said. "Dedication to his craft."

After that we walked over to Salem Common, which wasn't so far away. Michelle found a heated gazebo where we could sit together, watching some geese peck at the frosty grass. It was a wonder they hadn't flown south already.

"Didn't you ever want to be like Indiana Jones when you were little?" Michelle asked.

"No," I said.

"I did," Michelle said. "But then kids change dreams so much when they're little. I started wanting to be a ballerina when I was nine. I'd love it if I were good enough to make the American Ballet Theatre company. I'm not, though."

"How can you be sure about that?"

Michelle shrugged with a little smile. "There are other girls in my class who are just as good as me. Even better."

"You're being modest," I said.

"I'm not. We can't all be the best at everything we do."

"Even if you're right about there being better dancers, what makes you think those are the girls who want to be career bal-lerinas? Some of them are practicing it for fun. They'll grow up and become bankers and programmers and stay-at-home moms. It's not the most talented people who go on to be the most successful at something. It's the ones who don't stop try-ing until there's nothing left for them to do but succeed."

"You get that gem of wisdom from Adrian Doherty?" Michelle asked, grinning impishly.

"Don't know what gave it away," I said, grinning back.

Our smiles faded. We spent some time looking around the park, at the people riding by on bikes and Segways.

"It's not right," Michelle said quietly. "Your parents making you live like this. If you were transgender and they were keeping you off of hormones . . ."

"But I'm not transgender," I said. I was something in-between, something most people didn't know existed.

"I don't see how it's very different," Michelle said. "You're a boy. But because you get your period sometimes, they're saying you're a girl. Have you ever felt even a little like a girl?"

I shook my head.

"I know your body is considered female, but it's also male. I don't understand how they can ignore that half of you."

"It must be easier for them, somehow," I said. In the history of mankind, we always chose the easiest route, not the kindest one. I'd read a statistic once that said 60 percent of doctors didn't wash their hands properly because it cost them extra time between patients. Their dirty hands contributed to open wound infections that caused between twenty and fifty thousand preventable deaths a year.

"When does this end, though?" Michelle asked. "You can't pretend to be something you're not forever."

"I don't know," I admitted, feeling hollow. "I guess until college. Then they can't make me pretend."

"That's two years away!"

She moved closer until we were sitting on the same side of the gazebo. She was right next to me, so close that our knees touched through our jeans.

"Tell a doctor," Michelle begged. "Tell *somebody*."

Which doctor was I supposed to tell about this? Dr. Tran, who was all jazzed up about the potential that I could have vagina babies someday? Look what happened when teachers found out. They didn't know how to handle someone like me because this was the first time they'd had to deal with someone like me. Yeah, well, this was the first time I'd had to deal with me too. I couldn't go around teaching people when I was still learning myself.

Michelle pulled me into a hug. I almost fell on her, but planted my hands on the seat to keep from crushing her. She was tiny, but it felt like she surrounded me. She was warm. And she was shaking, which I couldn't attribute solely to the cold.

"Don't let them kill you," Michelle begged. "Don't let them kill my best friend."

I wanted to be more than her best friend. If I were a normal guy, I would've tested the waters by now. The problem was, I didn't know for sure what she saw when she looked at me. She said she was my friend regardless of my sex. I could buy that, but that was a world away from being comfortable dating someone who was both sexes. And even if she was comfortable with that, there was absolutely no reason she had to be attracted to me.

And if she was attracted to me? Well, it would still be a risk for her to get too close to me. To attract people's attention and judgment and suspicion, more than we already did. We were the Contemporary Witches of Salem, after all. Two outcasts unable to blend in, unable to fit the mold. The kind of people you blamed when the social order got disturbed, when the rye grew mold and rotted people's brains. I didn't need to be a historian or an anthropologist to know that three centuries wasn't long enough to change human behavior.

11

One day at the start of March, Miss Marbury stopped me on my way out of history class.

"Do you have a few minutes to talk after school today?" she asked.

My stomach turned at the thought that I might be in trouble—though I couldn't think of anything bad I'd done yet. She didn't ask for my mother to be there, so that was probably a good sign.

"Just ten minutes?" Miss Marbury asked. "Out by the Zen garden, if that works for you."

"Okay," I said. "I'll text my mom."

Salem was already yielding to spring. Leaves were starting to curl open on the tips of the trees, but they hadn't spread out yet, the branches left bare. Dewy moss crawled up the sides of the trunks. In a few weeks' time, we'd probably switch to the short-sleeved uniform.

In the Zen garden, I sat down on a bench warmed by the sun and watched coppery carp plashing in the noisy pond. Miss Marbury came and sat next to me, rubbing her arms, even though I didn't think it was that cold out.

"How are you liking it here?" she asked.

Had Mom put her up to this? "It's fine," I said.

"You know the Hawthorne Hotel in the historic district?

Every year around this time, they hold a paranormal convention. Ghost hunters come to talk about their findings. Do you believe in things like that?"

"Not really," I said. "But I know people are always saying that old hotel is haunted." I thought it was confirmation bias at work. Somebody tells you your hotel room is haunted, you forget you left the faucet on overnight, and in the morning, you've got proof a specter visited you.

"Nathaniel Hawthorne was related to Judge John Hathorne," Miss Marbury said. "He was so embarrassed by the part his ancestor played in the witch trials that he changed the spelling of his name to distance himself from it. And it must have worked. We remember him for his great writing, not for his relation to a mass murderer."

I wasn't sure why she had called me out here to talk. If it was just about history, I'd have preferred that she keep the lessons confined to school.

She stretched her legs out in front of her, her hands on her knees. I didn't have it in me to interrupt her; with her guileless, sheeplike face, no one would have.

"My ancestor was one of the witch trial victims too," Miss Marbury said. "Her name was Rebecca Nurse. She was in her seventies, and her death was unprecedented. She was a beloved woman of such good standing that when she was accused, the whole village went down to the courthouse to defend her. It was the first inkling many people had that things had gone too far. But there was nothing they could do at that point. The judges weren't keen to give up their power."

"Nobody is, once they've tasted it," I said.

Miss Marbury looked me in the eye. "I'm sorry if I'm being rude," she said—which I could hardly believe, because I'd never once heard a teacher apologize to a student, even when the teacher was in the wrong. "And I'm sorry if it seems that I'm prying. But Principal Eaton let the staff know about your condition."

"Oh." What else could I really say?

"Are you okay?" she asked. "Is anyone bothering you here?"

"It's fine," I said. "I haven't told my classmates about me." I felt a sudden flash of panic. "You're not going to, are you?"

"Oh, no," she said, wide-eyed, like she had never considered such a thing. "No, I would never."

That was what she said, at least. I didn't know if she would hold true to that.

"I just don't want you to think there's anything wrong with you," Miss Marbury said. "Even if that's what people have told you before. You're different, but if everyone would stop and be honest with themselves, we'd realize that we all have something that makes us different from one another."

"I'm not sure I believe that," I muttered.

"I had eleven fingers when I was born," Miss Marbury said.

I looked at her hands and only saw ten.

"My parents had it removed when I was little," Miss Marbury said. "That was what parents did back then with abnormalities. But I think nowadays, many parents are more progressive. They leave the choice for cosmetic electives up to their children."

My parents did leave the choice of my gender to me—right up until my body started hinting at the possibility of a different one. Was there something about periods that made people feel entitled to a girl's body? Even if that girl's body was really a boy's body? While I was thinking all this, Miss Marbury seemed to notice something was the matter; she looked at me closely, then quietly said, "Was I wrong?"

Michelle thought I should tell somebody about what I was feeling. Was this the right time to do it?

"Do you get the chance to go out to Boston much, Ashley?" Miss Marbury asked before I could decide whether to say anything. "I found a couple of intersex support groups there when I was doing some research over the weekend. Salem is very small, so I don't know if you'll get the support system you need here. You might consider asking your parents to take you out that way. It's not very far. You could make a day trip of it."

Evie lived in Boston. That alone meant my parents would never be willing to take me there. Besides, I could picture Dad grumbling the whole car ride about how much trouble I was being. Why couldn't I just shut up and be okay with everything?

"Here's the list," Miss Marbury said brightly, taking a folded piece of paper out of her purse. "And my contact information is on it too, in case you ever need it."

"Thanks," I said. I glanced at the paper—saw that she lived on Winter Street, not far from here—then folded it into a smaller square and stuffed it in my book bag. I wasn't sure what I was feeling.

◆◆◆

Tyler Morning was a pretty decent guy. Now that the Major League Soccer season had officially begun, he wanted to talk about almost nothing else. Nobody in my house liked soccer, and Corey had never liked it, either, so this was the first time I got to enjoy the sport as a co-spectator and not a player. I started getting Mom to take me early to school every day so we could have a few minutes before classes to discuss our favorite hopefuls. We were both huge fans of the New England Revolution—like we would dare to root for any other team—and now that they were about to announce new contracts, we were getting excited.

"Hand to God, I met Steve Nicol once," Tyler swore, having followed me to my locker. I stuffed my unneeded books inside.

"You're full of shit," I said. "That guy's ancient."

"Uh, no, he's only about sixty," Tyler said with an incredulous laugh. "But I think he moved back to the UK after he retired over here."

"Okay, then when did you meet him, big shot?"

"At a pub in Boston. I was eight."

"Your parents took their eight-year-old to a pub?"

"That's just what people do over there to unwind."

"You know Firmino? Guy was like seventeen when they signed him last year. Just think; that could've been any one of us."

"Well, not you," said Tyler, with another one of his baffled laughs.

It took me a moment.

"You're so cool," Tyler said. "You know? You're the only girl I've ever met who's this into soccer."

I felt something inside of me break a little. "Yeah. Thanks."

I stopped coming to school early after that.

◆◆◆

If there was any reason I wished I were still attending Deodat Lawson, it was Michelle, only Michelle. I'd taken for granted how much going to school together had facilitated our hanging out afterward. Now, instead of things just naturally falling into place, we had to plan them out in advance.

We decided to hang out on Friday, and because her ballet practice was going to run late that day, I told her I'd meet her there. The ballet studio was on Essex Street, like most things in our town were. When I stopped inside, girls in singlets were lined up before the mirrored wall, leaning against a wooden rail and swinging their legs around their heads like they were made of rubber. I had no idea how they managed it.

I spotted Michelle toward the back of the group. She stood on the very points of her toes, like she was weightless. It must have been agony to learn how to do that. She'd told me once that the very first dancer to develop that technique did it without any shoes at all. Why did humans subject themselves to so much pain in the name of beauty?

When Michelle stretched her arm out, like the neck of a graceful swan, she really was beautiful. She was beautiful all the time, but seeing her commit herself to something that fueled her made her more beautiful than most people looked on a runway. I felt a sudden, burning ache in the middle of my chest. I really liked her. Maybe I loved her, if I wasn't too selfish to know how such a thing was done. I wanted her to have everything she wanted out of life, even if it didn't benefit anybody else, even if I wouldn't be there to enjoy it. I wanted her to be safe. I didn't know what that was if it wasn't love.

When class was over, Michelle bounded over to me. "Hey, Ash!" she said, pulling her sweater on over her pink singlet and stepping into her street shoes. She was sweaty, and it was cold outside; I worried she might catch a fever. I held her coat out for her and she slipped into it. We left together.

"Where do you want to go?" Michelle asked.

"Wanna eat?" I asked. "Bet you're hungry, after all that exercise."

We walked a couple of blocks out to Bridge Street and went inside the Pickled Pearl. The curved wooden walls, some with portholes, made the place look like a pirate's ship. The front counter was even designed to resemble a prow with a figurehead. All the chairs were shaped like crates and barrels, all the tables like ship's wheels. We ordered sandwiches and sat down, while a busty wench with a stuffed parrot on her shoulder serenaded us.

"The people here sure are colorful," Michelle giggled when the waitress had gone.

At the next table over, three middle-aged women wore real pointed witches' hats. Nothing about their body language indicated that they were in costume.

"Salem's the home of freaks and weirdos," I said. Somehow I was the freakiest of all. Maybe my freak flag was different because I couldn't take it down at the end of the day.

Michelle seemed to follow my train of thought. She dragged a couple of her fries through a puddle of tartar sauce. She said, "You know, I know what it's like to be singled out too, Ash. Remember how Matthew Sommerheim used to torment me?"

I felt myself flush. Of course Michelle had firsthand experience with being treated like crap.

"Sommerheim's a jerk," was all I could manage to say.

"You know he asked me out last year?"

"What?" I felt like hunting him down and beating his face in.

Michelle shook her head. "Just because I grew up and got sort of pretty, he thought I'd forget all the times he bullied me in middle school."

"You didn't get 'sort of' pretty," I said.

"Okay, I get it, I'm a troll," Michelle said, grinning.

I told myself to cool it before I got carried away. We ate the rest of our meal while getting into a long conversation about which Skeletronics member we wished we could hang out with for a day.

Then we walked back to her house and holed ourselves up in her room to play a video game. We sat on the bed with the controllers on our laps, the title screen flashing on her TV. I was sure the game was good, but I was more preoccupied with the scent of Michelle's strawberry body wash, the sound of her fingertips tapping on the buttons. The worst kind of longing was when the person you wanted was right next to you, but you knew you couldn't have them.

During a cut-scene, I thought back to what Michelle had said in the restaurant. "Do other people here give you crap for being Black? Besides Sommerheim, I mean?"

She stretched her skinny arms over her head in a soundless yawn. "It was worse when I was little," she said. "But it's going to happen sometimes, isn't it? Especially when you think about how entrenched Salem is in its history, and how Black people first came here."

That was true, I reflected. Tituba and Mary Black and Candy were all enslaved Black women, and they were all accused of witchcraft—fodder for the cannons when God broke his covenant.

"I don't know why Matthew Sommerheim thought I'd go out with him. I guess I was supposed to feel lucky that he showed me attention. But if I dated somebody, he would have to be really kind. Even if he's sort of prickly on the surface, that's all right."

None of this was what I wanted to hear. It was kind of hurting me, but at the same time, I was interested. "That doesn't make sense. How can you be prickly *and* kind?"

"Well," she said, "he could be the cold, headstrong type who doesn't smile much, but he holds girls' hands when he finds them crying."

I had to be hearing her wrong. She was looking at the TV screen, not at me, washed out blues and whites reflected in the mirrors of her eyes.

"What the hell?" I said, just to get her attention.

"Oh, come on," she said, pausing the game. "You had to have known. I was crazy about you all during middle school!"

"How was I supposed to know that?"

"Wasn't it obvious? My mom said it was obvious."

"She's your mom. That's different."

I could have kicked Younger Me for being so oblivious. He had missed his chance, and now I was the one who had to suffer for it. I didn't even know what to say. Michelle was wrapping the cord around her controller, still not looking at me. Finally I said, "Well, I'm crazy about you now. So where does that get me?"

My mouth and my brain were pretty far divorced from each other.

Michelle peeked at me. Again, she looked away. She was smiling in a way I took to be either secretive or shy, her glasses sliding down her nose.

But then she said, "This is all wrong."

"What?" I asked, crestfallen.

"Just the way it's happening. I always had this idea that it'd be dark out, and 'Corroding with You' by the Skeletronics would be playing."

"Not 'Slaying the Metal Dragon'?" I asked, concentrating on sounding calm as the relief and the thrill of what she was saying sank in.

"'Corroding with You' is more romantic!"

"You could turn your light off, if it helps," I suggested. Even as I was thinking on a loop, *This is real, this is really happening, this is real.*

So she did. Her room didn't have a window, because the really old houses had them in the corridors, not the bedrooms. The only light in the room came from the paused video game.

She pulled her legs up on the bed so she was sitting on her knees, facing me. Her hair made a frizzy halo around her head.

"Even knowing what I am?" I asked, scared.

Michelle tucked her hair behind her ears, a pink glow about her face. "You're just a guy," she said. "And if you weren't, I'd still like you."

"But are you sure . . ."

"Shh," Michelle said.

I thought she was going to kiss me. But like a dork—an absolutely wonderful and perfect dork—she sang the chorus from her favorite song. It didn't even have words; it was just a bunch of rhythmic crooning. I sat and waited patiently for the nerd to get through with her ritual, swaying side to side. Then I moved in.

I'd kissed people before. Michelle hadn't. It was obvious, the tentative touch of mouth on mouth and the way she hesitated, awaiting instruction, until I gave it to her. For my part, I just couldn't believe I got to do this with her. I touched her hair, remembering the time she told me where her curls came from: "It's called a twist-out, Ash, use Google sometime." It was soft, and so were her lips, and the blanket underneath us, and I was so happy I didn't know how it was allowed, how it wasn't all a part of some joke.

12

April 14 was an important day for me—mainly because the New England Revolution were playing FC Dallas at Gillette Stadium. Last year, Dallas had flattened us, so I was looking forward to some sweet revenge. Mom didn't like me staying up late to watch sports on a school night, though, so I figured I'd have to sneak the coverage on my phone.

I'd just finished my breakfast when she surprised me with tickets to the game.

"Mom—are you serious?" I asked, awed. "This is all the way in Foxborough."

"It's only an hour away," Mom said. "That's plenty of time for me to drop off you and a couple of friends."

"But why?"

"It's your birthday, isn't it?"

That was the other reason April 14 was meaningful to me. Today was the day I turned seventeen. It was hard to believe it had been seven whole months since my body had started acting out of whack.

"You know, you're an Aries," Mom said. "That's why you have such a willful personality. Aries are very stubborn."

Someone was taking Salem's interest in all things occult a little too seriously.

Mom had given me three tickets to the game, which

sounded like a lot, but this early in the soccer season, they were dirt cheap. Or they were for an adult with a full-time job, anyway. Taking Michelle with me was a given. In the past, I would have brought Corey, too, or at least invited him, but we hadn't spoken since Christmas.

At school that morning, I asked Tyler if he'd like to come.

"Are you kidding?" he asked, his eyes lighting up. "That'd be sweet! Is it just the two of us?"

"Nah," I said. "My girl—my best friend's gonna be there. And my mom's probably gonna make me keep texting her to make sure I haven't been chopped up and murdered."

"Chopped up before murdered?"

"Watch *Braveheart*."

To get there in time, we were going to have to leave right after school. Mom picked the two of us up, then drove out to Michelle's place and picked her up too. Michelle climbed in the back seat with me, a big plastic bag on her lap.

"What's that?" I asked, grinning.

"Snacks and drinks to smuggle in," she said. "Refreshments are so expensive at basketball stadiums."

"Michelle," I said, "it's a soccer stadium."

"I know, but it can't be all that different. Don't worry. I packed your pork rinds."

"You like pork rinds?" Tyler asked.

"Yeah," I said. "Why?"

"I've never known any girls who like pork rinds."

I bit my tongue and said, "Maybe you never asked them."

Gillette Stadium was massive—it had a seating capacity of sixty thousand—and even with fewer than half the seats filled, the noise was deafening. I watched the Revs run out on the green in navy and white and saw their faces magnified on the jumbotrons. I yelled myself hoarse.

Nicolas Firmino was a powerhouse. He was only the fifth guy to join the team who was actually from Massachusetts, which said a lot about the way professional sports worked. He played midfielder, which some said wasn't as important as forward, because midfielders didn't score as many goals. But without them, there was nothing unifying offense and defense; in a way, you were expected to play both. It was a thankless, intricate juggling act. Besides, Ronaldo was a midfielder. Case closed.

I watched Firmino pass to Mancienne and felt a twinge of jealousy. These days, I was finally reconciling myself to the reality that that was never going to be me. What were you supposed to do when you woke up one day and found out your dreams weren't coming true? Millions of people went through this, but there was no real guidebook for it. I told myself now wasn't the time to mope. The coolest girl in the world was sitting next to me, drinking hot cocoa from a thermos. At least one dream had come true. Some people weren't even that lucky.

Tyler acted like a prick throughout the match. I didn't know what was the matter with him, but if I didn't react to an unfunny joke he made, or if I paid more attention to Michelle than to him, he shut down and lapsed into a moody silence. This wasn't a goddamn popularity contest. Besides, he never bothered asking Michelle the most cursory of questions, like where she went to school or how long we had known each other.

That was when I realized that just because you have an interest in common with a person doesn't mean you're really friends. And it sucked, because I missed having guy friends to shoot the breeze with. Girls were awesome, but they were girls. They didn't understand a lot of things we did, like why we said we were going to call when we had no intention (didn't want to hurt their feelings), or why we were constantly moving our junk around (that shit moved itself).

I decided not to hang out with Tyler so much. But as it happened, he planned to see more of me than I was comfortable with.

●●●

It happened the next day, when I was getting ready to leave school. Tyler caught me in the hall and asked if we could talk for a second.

Now that the weather had warmed up, I was legging it back to Summer Street every day. I liked long walks; they gave me time alone with my own thoughts. But if it was only five minutes, I could wait a bit. We went inside the empty math classroom. It was one of the few without windows, and he closed the door behind us and didn't turn the lights on. It took a second for my eyes to adjust.

"I like you," Tyler said. "You're so cool—you're a girl, but you're like one of the guys."

I suppressed an eye roll. "Thanks, Tyler."

All of a sudden, he was coming at me. Trying to kiss me.

I forced my hands between us, shoving him back. My heart was racing with fear. What the fuck was that? Who just *did* something like that?

"Come on," Tyler said, frustrated.

"Come on what? What the fuck is wrong with you?"

Tyler stared at me, like he really didn't get it. "I thought you were into me."

"What the *fuck* made you think that?"

"What about all the times you hung out with me?"

"To talk about soccer, not because I thought you were hot!"

Tyler had the nerve to look hurt.

"What about Naia?" I asked, enraged for her. "You know, your girlfriend?"

"What about her?" Tyler asked. "If you'd go out with me, I'd dump her."

There weren't words for how livid I was. You didn't *do* that to a person.

And now what? Now that I'd rejected him, was he going to pretend to Naia that nothing had happened? It was funny that I was angrier for her than I was for me. As I thought about her, I went silent. Tyler took it for consent and tried to kiss me again.

It was gratifying to learn that five months out of practice, I still had my soccer reflexes. I kicked him in the dick. Hard. He shouted with pain and sprawled into one of the desks, knocking it out of its row. The chair fell over with a hard crash. I turned my back on him and left him there.

◆◆◆

Overnight, my anger toward Tyler cooled down to a sadness. Now that I knew what he really wanted from me, I found myself reviewing every conversation we'd ever had. Here I was thinking he liked me as a friend, as a person, but he only liked what he thought was in my pants.

Had I ever done to some girl what Tyler had done to me? Had Louisa Carmichael wanted a friend in tenth grade, but settled for dating when I never considered anything else?

Michelle was my friend first. If we ever broke up, we would probably still be friends. I couldn't bear the thought of breaking up with her, though. I couldn't imagine liking her any less than I did here and now.

When I went to school on Wednesday, I worried people would treat me differently. If Tyler went around telling our classmates I'd socked him in the nads, it might start real trouble for me.

I worried for no reason. In the hallways and the classrooms, nobody looked at me twice. He must have been embarrassed that a girl had beaten him up.

There was still one problem: I didn't know what to do about Naia. Because if nobody else knew about our confrontation, that meant Naia didn't, either. If I told her what her boyfriend had done, it might mean hurting her. She was the first person in this school to treat me nicely.

Even taking all that into account, I felt that I had to tell her the truth. Tyler was lying to her by stringing her along, acting like he wanted to be with her when he just wanted to be with somebody, period. And if he'd been willing to mess around with me behind her back, it was only a matter of time before he tried it again with someone else. I resolved to find her and break it to her, even though the idea of it tied my stomach into knots.

I wasn't able to get her alone until right before third period. Ironically, we were in the girls' bathroom when I found her.

"Hey," I said. "Can we talk?"

She dried her hands at the sink, wadding up the brown paper towel. "Sure we can, Ash. Is everything okay?"

I blurted out, "Tyler tried to kiss me yesterday."

Naia stared at me without changing expression.

"I kicked him in the dick," I said. "So if he's been limping around you lately—"

"You expect me to believe that?"

I was the one who stared this time. "What?"

"Let me guess. You came onto him, but he turned you

down. Now you're pissed off, and you're trying to start problems between us."

The sadness boiled back up to anger. "If you seriously think I would be interested in that prick, you're delusional."

"Whatever you say, princess."

It didn't matter what I thought. It didn't matter what the truth was. By lunchtime, all Naia's friends were giving me dirty looks. I sat alone, while Naia and Tyler sat together at a crowded table. She leaned against his shoulder while he kissed the top of her head. He caught me looking his way and quickly shifted his gaze. I went on glowering at him, knowing he could feel it. There were few things I hated more than cowards. Liars were pretty high up there.

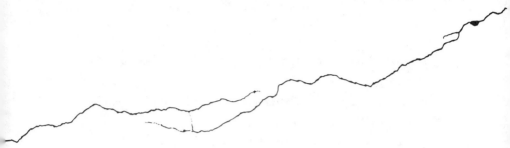

13

If it was a choice between the reliable class rep everyone had gone to school with for years and the weird transfer student with the deep voice and scruffy hair, the choice was an obvious one. I wasn't surprised when girls stopped talking to me and started shooting me hostile looks instead. I could deal with the loneliness. I only had to hang on until June.

I could deal with the loneliness because I had Michelle. We talked on the phone every night, sometimes just to listen to music together. But on a Friday at the end of April, she didn't call me at our regularly scheduled time. I started to worry that something had happened to her. That was when I heard the doorbell ring. When I went downstairs to answer it, she was on the other side.

"What?" I asked. "Is everything okay?"

Michelle threw her arms around my neck with a sigh. "My parents are fighting again. This time it's really bad. Can I stay here with you?"

I let her inside, closing the door. "You mean for the night?" I asked uncertainly.

"If that's okay," Michelle said. She dug her fingers into my side. "Your mom's making you act like you're a girl, right? So if you have a sleepover with a girl, she can't say anything about it."

It was deceitful, but totally brilliant of her. I tried to find

Mom to tell her about it, but the only person home was Dad. He grunted at me—his way of saying "Do whatever you want, I don't care"—and went right back to watching CNN. Michelle followed me upstairs to my room.

"What happened?" I asked, closing the door.

"It's about ballet," Michelle said. "Mom thinks it's too much money and wants to stop paying for it. Dad said she was being ridiculous, and then she said I wasn't even good at it—"

"She's out of her mind!"

"Oh, Ash, sometimes I swear she regrets it. Every time she gets mad at me, or I do something I'm not supposed to, she looks at me in this quiet way, and I know she's thinking about how my sister might not have behaved like me. She even said it once, after she'd been drinking. I don't know if she remembers."

"Wait here," I said. "I'm gonna make you something that'll make you feel better."

"Marshmallow and potato chip sandwiches?" Michelle asked shyly.

"What else?"

They were disgusting, but she loved them. Considering my pork rind habit, I didn't think I had room to judge. I went down to the kitchen and made her a couple of sandwiches. When I went back upstairs with them, she was playing *Salem Online* on her phone.

"I just played a game with somebody named Deodab Lawdank," Michelle said. "See that? You've got a bunch of fans, and you didn't even know."

"They're not fans," I said, handing her the plate. "They probably don't remember I'm the one who messed with the sign."

"So modest," she teased.

We stayed up late, eating junk food, watching Animal Planet, and lip-synching to the Skeletronics. Mom still hadn't come home, but that happened sometimes. Occasionally she had to stay late at the physical office to manage bookings, especially when her manager had accidentally booked two different tour groups at the same time. When night fell, the topic turned to what Michelle was going to wear to bed.

"I didn't even think," she said. "I just ran out of the house with the clothes on my back. Do you have anything I can borrow?"

"If you want to wear a T-shirt and boxers, sure," I said.

"That sounds fun," Michelle said cheerfully. "I've always thought boxers looked comfy."

So I gave her a pair, because why not? She went down the hall to the bathroom, then came back wearing them.

And honestly, she looked amazing, even with tiny hips drowning in all that loose fabric. Even the shirt was loose on her, sagging around her collarbone and pooling around her waist. She plodded over to the bed and sat down on it, stifling a yawn.

"Oh no," she said suddenly.

"What?" Had she caught me staring?

"I left my scarf at home," Michelle said.

"Your scarf?" It was April.

"The one I wrap my hair in at night so it doesn't break." She groaned. "It's gonna look like such a mess tomorrow morning . . ."

I wasn't really sure I understood, but if it was important to her, it was important to me. The last thing I wanted was for her to feel uncomfortable here. "I probably have a scarf around here somewhere."

"No, it needs to be silk," Michelle said, "or at least something cheap that feels like it."

"Can you get something like that at the drugstore?"

"Well—"

"I'll go get you one," I said.

"No, Ash, you don't have to do that!"

"It's not a problem."

I grabbed a jacket out of my closet and left the house. Salem looked peaceful and sleepy by night, the windows of the ancient houses all lit up. With so few cars on the street, I could almost pretend I was back in the 1600s and the burning lights were from candlewicks. At the drugstore, the clerk was amused when I asked her for help but pointed out the headscarves for natural hair. The boxes said the scarves were made of satin. For $8.99, I had my doubts.

Back in my room, Michelle lay on her side on the bed, sleeping. She must have tried her hardest to stay awake, because *Tituba: A Biography* was open across her hip. I sat on the edge of the bed and shoulder gently. "Mich. Scarf's here."

"Hmm?"

She rubbed her cheek on the bed, slowly coming to. Then she went to the bathroom with the scarf. When she came back, her abundance of curls was missing in action and the black scarf was knotted cutely at the top of her head. She climbed back into bed, taking off her glasses.

"Good night," she said. "Don't hog the blankets."

"They're my blankets," I retorted as I turned off my lamp. "I can hog them if I want."

I won't lie and say it didn't make me nervous to sleep in the same bed as her. But we'd been friends since we were kids, so maybe that took some of the edge off of it. I couldn't see her in the dark, but that didn't stop me from feeling comforted by her presence. I could sense the warmth radiating off of her, hear her breath stirring the bedsheets.

When I woke up the next morning, Michelle was still out like a light. My bedroom door was ajar; I didn't remember leaving it open. I got dressed, went to the bathroom to wash up, and dragged myself downstairs in search of something to eat.

Mom was sitting in the kitchen, hands wrapped around her coffee mug. I knew perfectly well there wasn't coffee in there, but cranberry juice. Mom got so many UTIs, she didn't bother visiting doctors for them anymore.

I'm sure I said hello, but she didn't answer me, not until I'd taken the toaster off the top of the refrigerator.

"When did Michelle come over?" Mom asked.

I put the toaster on the counter. "Last night. She just wanted to sleep over."

"And you thought that was okay?"

My skin was prickling in warning. "Why wouldn't it be? We're both 'girls,' right?"

Mom put the mug down with a clink.

"I'm going upstairs," I said.

"No, you're not," Mom said. Usually she was never this direct with me. "I don't think you should be seeing Michelle anymore."

My blood thundered treacherously in my ears. "What?"

Mom sipped the last of her cranberry juice.

"Why can't I see Michelle, Mom?" I asked, getting heated. "Don't you want me to be a girl? Aren't girls supposed to have friends who are girls?"

Mom put the mug down. "You found a way to be worse than your sister," she said quietly. "You couldn't just be disgusting with another girl. You had to do it with a black girl."

She might as well have slapped me across the face. "What did you just say?" I asked, stunned.

"I think you should tell her to go home," Mom said. "Her parents must be missing her."

It was Mom's house. If she wanted Michelle to go, then what I wanted didn't matter. But I couldn't believe what I was hearing. It was like my mom had transformed into an ugly, slime-oozing cryptid overnight. Or maybe that monster had been there all along, and I'd been blind to it—because for so many years, I'd been the only target of its malice.

❧❧❧

I made up my mind not to tell Michelle about Mom's racist comment. But I decided to tell her the other parts. After Michelle had gone home, I holed myself up in my room and called her to talk about the argument.

"But you're a boy," Michelle said quietly. "It shouldn't matter what gender you are, but if she's determined to make a big thing out of it . . . you're a boy."

"I don't know what's going on," I said. My voice was climbing without my say. Even I could hear the panic ringing in it. "Why won't she listen to me? Why won't anyone listen to me?"

"You need to tell someone, Ash." She'd made this argument before. "If your teachers won't listen, tell a doctor. If your doctor won't listen—"

"Who do I tell? A priest?"

We both paused to consider the absurdity. Historically, religious leaders in Salem didn't have a terrific track record when it came to people who fell outside the norm.

Michelle stayed silent on the other end. I heard her parents yelling and figured they might be arguing again. Then she said, "Ash? I've got to go. Mom wants me."

"Okay," I said. "Call me when you get the chance."

I waited a couple of hours to see if she would call me back. When she didn't, I figured the shouting match must have been especially bad this time. To pass the time, I browsed Reddit and played a couple of games of *Salem Online*.

At two o'clock, Mom called me downstairs. I trudged into the dining room, expecting another argument.

Michelle's parents were sitting at the table with Mom and Dad. Mrs. Carrier had a face too heavy for her thin frame, her graying hair pulled back in a puffy bun. Mr. Carrier's goatee and soul patch, fighting for dominance on his face, rivaled the facial hair of Anton LaVey himself. I hated comparing Michelle's dad to the founder of the Church of Satan. I only knew about that guy because we had a Satanic Temple here in Salem and the two branches of Satanists were constantly fighting with each other.

Michelle was sitting at the table too. She looked smaller than usual, shrinking in on herself like a beaten puppy. She was staring so hard at the table I wondered if she was trying to burn holes through it.

"Wow," I said, grabbing a seat. "Looking like a regular witches' Sabbath here."

"Hello, Ashley," Mrs. Carrier said. The kindness in her voice didn't reach her eyes. "How are you?"

I stared back at her. "Fine," I said shortly. Now that I knew the kinds of things she said to her daughter, I didn't care to make an impression.

"Ashley," Mr. Carrier said. He put his elbows on the table, his long fingers folded together. "We've all been talking."

"Pretty sure I gathered that on my own," I said.

"You're a nice kid," Mr. Carrier said. "We've known you for a long time now. But you're not what we want for our daughter.

We think she's getting confused, because of the way you used to present."

"The way I . . . ?"

"When you were dressing like a boy," he began, but that was as far as he got before my dad interrupted him.

"You're not seeing each other anymore," Dad said. "Say your goodbyes and get it over with."

It felt like a buzz saw was cutting into my chest. I could practically hear the ragged noise it made, back and forth, back and forth. "She's been my best friend for ages!" I said.

This wasn't fair, I thought, looking around at their faces. How couldn't they see that?

Michelle made a sound, the first one she'd made in a while. "W-What if we were just friends? What if we didn't go out together? Wouldn't that be okay?"

Mr. Carrier's jaw tightened. "We've talked about this, Michelle."

"But he's m-my best friend. I don't want to stop talking to him. Please . . ."

"That's another thing," Mr. Carrier said. "We want you to start making friends with normal girls. This isn't what you should be subjected to at your age."

"Hold up," Dad said. "What do you mean, normal?"

"I mean no offense," Mr. Carrier said, lifting his hands in surrender.

"Sure sounded like you did," Dad said. "Guess we can't all be father of the year like you." I understood at once that he wasn't offended on my behalf. He was offended that his parenting was being called into question.

"Look, as long as we're in agreement on everything else," Mr. Carrier said.

"Yeah, we're in agreement that you're a shithead," Dad said.

Mr. Carrier squared his jaw again. He stood up. "Girls, we're leaving." Then he looked at me. "Don't let me catch you around my daughter again."

I looked at Michelle and saw that tears were silently streaming down her face. That was the worst part. How could these people pretend that they loved her, but hurt her until she cried? I was supposed to be the one who was bad for her to be around, and I would rather have run out into traffic than do anything I thought might make her sad.

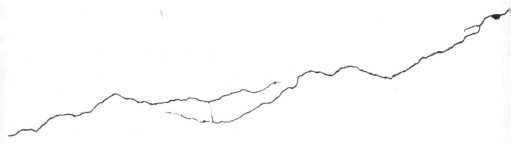

14

If anyone thought I'd cut Michelle out of my life just because I was under orders to do just that, they didn't know me. I gave things a day to cool down, then sent her a text message. All it said was, **i'm still here**. We might not be able to see each other physically, but I needed her to know I wasn't giving up on her.

You can tell when a person leaves your message on read. Corey and I used to bitch at each other all the time for doing it, but I'd never once done that to Michelle, and she'd never done that to me. A couple of hours after I texted her, there was a check mark next to the message, letting me know she'd seen it. But she still hadn't responded.

Maybe she was just waiting to get away from her parents. It was no big deal, I told myself. Considering recent events, they were probably watching her with eagle eyes. If she wanted to talk to me without them knowing about it, she'd have to wait for the right opportunity.

As late as seven o'clock that night, there was no reply from her.

I started to get worried. Because as far as I could see, there were only two possibilities. Either Michelle had read my text and she didn't plan on answering me, or one of her parents had read the text and was keeping her phone from her. If it was the latter, she might be in trouble just because

I'd tried contacting her. If it was the former . . . what did that mean? I couldn't blame her if she wanted to keep the peace with her parents. They were the ones she had to live with. Or had she read my text and then had her phone confiscated? Should I try contacting her again, or should I leave things alone?

If Michelle's crying was the worst part of all this, the uncertainty was the second worst. I couldn't just pop over to her house to find out what was going on, and now that we went to different schools, I couldn't ask our mutual friends. All I could do was wonder if she was okay. It turned out that my imagination could conjure up some pretty bad punishments for her. Maybe she was locked in her room with the lights turned off, computer and TV unplugged. What if she was forbidden from talking to *all* her friends, not just me? I imagined she was just as alone as I was, and I wanted to scream.

◆◆◆

So texting was a dead end, but there were other ways I could try to get in touch with Michelle without her parents knowing. For starters, we both played *Salem Online*. I started signing on after school every day, hoping to catch her. But either we never signed on at the same time, or she just didn't feel like playing the game anymore.

I had her email address. I registered a new one for myself, in case her parents had blocked mine, and sent her a letter without a subject. Days passed, and before I knew it, it was almost the weekend again, and she still hadn't replied.

And the reality finally dawned on me, finally settled in, that I was alone. It was over. Michelle was the one person still willing to spend time with me, who liked me without wanting or expecting something, who didn't think I was a freak because of the way I was born.

Now I didn't have a single person in the entire world on my side.

♦♦♦

It was summer in Salem. Oak trees canopied the sidewalks in swaths of leaf-shaped shadows, watery sunlight leaking through the branches. Tin wind chimes hung outside doors. The city-wide trolleys started running again. They only ever saw business now and around Halloween. Kids who were let out of school early made trips to Ye Olde Pepper Candy Companie on Essex Street to celebrate the end of the school term, which was never complete without a bag of warm, melt-in-your-mouth buttercrunch. As far as celebratory treats went, I preferred Red's Sandwiches. Michelle and Corey and I used to end our school year there. It was nothing more special than your run-of-the-mill greasy spoon. I loved it anyway. I used to buy cole-slaw and onion rings, the latter of which got snapped up so fast by my so-called friends that I had to order a second serving.

The last day of eleventh grade fell in early June. I didn't much feel like celebrating, but I thought I ought to do something to mark the start of summer anyway. After school, I walked out to the Salem Willows. The last time I had been there was almost a year ago, with Corey. Now I was alone, in a white blouse and a red skirt, with hair that fell past my chin and elastic bra straps digging into my back.

I walked under the shade of the willow trees and stopped next to the shore. Two men with fishing rods cast their lure a few feet away. A young, hapless mother chased her gurgling toddler across the sand. It was hard to remember that Salem was a nice place for most people to grow up. It was hard to remember that it had been nice for me.

It was probably nice for Bridget Bishop once too. She built two taverns from the ground up, after all. People wound up on her doorstep when they needed to fill their bellies and warm their skin. I bet they loved her once. All of that changed overnight for her, and I couldn't say it was much different for me.

"I am innocent," she said at her trial. "I know nothing of it. I have done no witchcraft. I am as innocent as the child unborn."

Why the fuck did we have to wear a white soccer uniform? Why couldn't it have been any other color?

After only ten minutes, I walked home from the beach. I was so tired, and my legs like lead; it took me twice as long as it usually did. At home, I went up to my room to take a nap. I had to pause halfway up the staircase; and when I did, I wondered how I had gotten here. I didn't remember any part of the school day. I didn't remember getting the results of my finals or saying goodbye to my teachers. It was strange. I was still thinking how strange it was when I lay down.

When I woke up from my nap, it was still light outside. The sun took longer to set during the summer. I went downstairs and found Mom sitting at the dining room table, looking through our mail. She took her reading glasses off and passed an envelope to me. She'd already opened it. The old me would have been indignant that she'd read my mail, but the new me was too tired to get angry anymore. I was too tired to think anything, much less feel.

I sat down at the table. Inside the envelope was a letter, written on loose leaf, folded into threes.

Dear Ash. The page was spotted with dried drops of moisture. *I never liked you, I just thought I did. I know now that it was wrong and I am sorry I misled you. We are both girls and it was wrong. Dad said I could write you one last letter. I am going for the summer to Indiana, where I will attend a summer school called God's Glory. They will teach me not to like girls and to be normal again. I'm sorry for the lies. Don't try to call me. Michelle.*

It was bullshit. Her father had probably been breathing down her neck, dictating her every word. I put the letter on the table. I didn't stuff it back in the envelope. I sat back in my chair, reviewing what I had read.

I laughed. Once I'd started, I couldn't stop. I laughed until I was dizzy, until I thought I would puke. I couldn't breathe. It was fucking hilarious. Holy shit. This was all so fucking absurd. I couldn't believe my life was like this.

"I'm tired," I said. "I'm going back to bed."

"Don't forget dinner," Mom said. "There's lasagna in the fridge."

♦♦♦

The next time I woke up, the time on my alarm clock read 12:22. It was after midnight. Altogether, I had slept nine hours. My pillow was spotted with sweat, making me wish my room had windows. I got up to use the bathroom and splash water on my face.

As I stepped out of the bathroom, I felt a heavy weight press down on my chest. My shoulders tingled, then the rest of my arms, spreading to my fingers. They numbed at the ends, so when I touched my face, I wasn't even sure they were making contact.

The second-floor catwalk was illuminated by the moonlight seeping in through the window. It tilted and lurched, which I thought was weird. Moonlight wasn't supposed to tilt and lurch. I realized I was falling. I hit the floor so hard that my knees banged against it like shots out of a cannon. I tried to yell but couldn't open my mouth. I couldn't move.

I wasn't sure how long I lay on the floor. I might have slipped back into sleep, because I saw things that couldn't possibly have been real. I saw my sister on her sixteenth birthday—the day our mother's mother, now deceased, gave her a used car for a gift. She climbed into the front seat, but unlike in the reality, I climbed in the passenger seat with her. We drove far, far away, laughing like we were in on the same joke. We almost made it out of Massachusetts, but a state trooper stopped us and asked for ID. He had to make sure we were both girls.

I woke up. I wasn't in my room, or in my house, but in a bed that felt thin underneath me, surrounded by clean white walls. There was a machine beside me, blocky and gray. I sat up. I was wearing a papery hospital gown with tiny gray elephants printed on the front. My ass felt bare and cold.

Nobody else was in the room. There was a button on the bed rail that said *ASSIST.* I could hear noises outside the far door—conversations and beeping equipment and the occasional laugh. I shouted, "Hey!" My voice was too hoarse to carry.

I had nothing to lose. I pressed the button.

A ginger-haired, broad-faced bear of a man stepped into the room in hospital scrubs. "You're up!" he said. "I'll give your parents a call."

"Why am I in the hospital?" I asked groggily.

"You passed out," the man said. "I'll wait until your parents are here so I don't have to explain everything twice. I'm Dr. Jacobs. You hungry?"

"No," I said. I was never hungry these days.

The man walked away. A couple of nurses made the rounds to check on me, along with an orderly carrying a tray of toast and foul-smelling gravy. I still wasn't hungry. Finally, about half an hour after I'd woken up, my parents rushed into the room, neither one meeting my eyes. They both grabbed one of the pleather visitor's chairs. Dad looked annoyed, checking the time on his phone.

"I brought a change of clothes for you," Mom said, clearly just to fill the silence. "They're in that locker behind your bed. Your phone too, though the charger's still at home somewhere . . ."

The red-haired doctor returned, sparing me from more empty chatter. "Well, her vitals look good," he said. "You're lucky you got her here right away. You must be relieved."

Nah, they probably weren't.

"What happened?" I asked. "Am I sick?"

Dr. Jacobs turned a chair around and sat in it backwards, his arms over the place his head should have gone. "You've got a condition called salt wasting," he said.

"What's that?" I asked.

"It's something that can happen with congenital adrenal hyperplasia. It means your body isn't retaining as much salt as it's supposed to. So what you get is fainting, lethargy, even seizures. Stress makes the symptoms worse. Over time, it gives you some pretty serious heart problems."

Heart problems? Like, I could actually die from this? I guess if you wish hard enough for something, it can come true.

"Wait a minute," Mom interrupted. "Isn't this something we should have known about when he—when she was very little?"

"Typically it would show up in the first few weeks of infancy," Dr. Jacobs agreed. "Except when it comes to a form of CAH called POR deficiency, where the symptoms present later in life. Ash might have been misdiagnosed at birth. We'd have to run a few more tests to make sure."

"But what makes all of this happen?" Dad asked, gesturing at me with his paw of a hand. He didn't waste a glance on me.

"It's basically because the mixed sex hormones are sending some confusing signals to Ashley's adrenal gland," Dr. Jacobs said. "The adrenal gland doesn't know how to interpret the signals, so it stops producing cortisol. Without cortisol, there's nothing in her body to absorb the salt it needs from nutrients."

"And how is that usually treated?" Mom asked.

"Cortisol injections," Dr. Jacobs said. "They'll help her body hold onto salt. Hormone replacement therapy helps stabilize the body too. Oh, and"—he shot me a grin I didn't return—"a junk food diet high in salty snacks doesn't hurt."

The pork rinds had actually been saving my goddamn life. What a trip.

A silence filled the room. Dad said, "How much does all that cost?"

"That's up to her insurance provider," Dr. Jacobs began. "But—"

"You told us she's got a testicle," Dad said. "Couldn't we just cut out the testicle?"

My head snapped in Dad's direction so suddenly, I heard my neck crack. "I have a testicle?"

He ignored me.

Dr. Jacobs said, "We found a testicle during X-rays, yes. It's in your inguinal canal."

"I have a testicle," I repeated. Nobody ever fucking told me. It felt like proof. I was a guy, no matter what they said about me, no matter what they told me I had to be. I was real. I was real. I was—

"If we have to lower her testosterone, or whatever," Dad said, "can't we just cut out the testicle? Seems to me that'd take care of the problem."

Jesus Christ. Even biology didn't convince them. I didn't know why I'd thought, even for a nanosecond, that it would. The testicle was just one more piece of evidence they were ready to discard, along with everything I'd ever done and said and thought my entire life.

They knew I was a boy, and they were forcing me to be a girl anyway. They were killing the person I really was because it was easier for them. My death was easier than my existence.

Dr. Jacobs paused. "I suppose we could try that," he said. "If that's what Ashley wants. I'm a little reluctant to recommend excising a healthy gonad, though."

"Don't undescended testicles cause cancer?" Mom asked.

"No, not necessarily," Dr. Jacobs said. "They're more likely than scrotal testicles to develop testicular cancer, that's true. But even with the risk factor, it's still a less than 1 percent chance that malignant cells develop. In Ashley's case, it's probably even lower, since her testicle produces no seminal fluid. We're discussing an invasive surgery. Ashley might prefer yearly monitoring instead."

"But if we don't correct this—this salt wasting thing, she'll die?"

Wasn't that what you wanted, Mom?

"Mrs. Bishop, there's no guarantee that testicular excision would bring Ashley's testosterone levels down to where we need them to be. I really recommend the cortisol shots. They're the conventional treatment for this condition."

"Shots for the rest of her life, or a one-time surgery," Dad muttered.

"*If* the surgery worked," Dr. Jacobs reminded him.

"I'm a guy," I said, gripping the bed railings. "I told you. I told you I'm a guy! Even my body says I'm a guy!"

It was poetic justice, I thought. They tried forcing me into a girl-shaped package, and my body rebelled—hard. It rebelled so damn hard it nearly killed me. At long last, I had an ally.

"Ashley!" Mom whispered. It was one of those loud whispers, the kind that defeats its own purpose.

Dr. Jacobs gave me a probing look. "Ashley, are you looking to transition? We can discuss that too if you'd like."

"She's just upset right now," Mom said. "Please! We'll talk about this at home."

"Of course you need to talk about it, but you need to talk about it right now. Again, Mrs. Bishop, this is a fatal condition if left unaddressed. I'll give you some privacy to think about your next step, okay? Page one of us when you're ready to proceed."

Dr. Jacobs left the room. I felt extraordinarily uncomfortable. It wasn't just that I was under scrutiny by my two worst enemies right now. My main problem was the clock. I had a limited amount of time to convince them I was a boy, and to let me go back to being the way I used to be. We couldn't just walk out of here and sit on it for a few days. I might actually die if we waited.

"Ashley . . ." Mom began, pleading.

"I'm a guy," I said. "I'm telling the doctor when he comes back."

"Please, don't do that," Mom said. "It's too hard! We—we had to explain to all our friends that our son was a girl now—it was so embarrassing—and now for you to say you want to go back the other way—"

"It was embarrassing for *you*?" I yelled. "You're not the one who got the shit beat out of you by your teammates! You're not the one who had to run home at the end of the day because you've needed to pee for the last six hours, and you're not allowed!"

"You're not thinking about us at all! You're only thinking about yourself!"

"I have to! I'm the only one who does it anymore!"

Dad finally looked at me. It was more like he looked through me, so cold and so hard that I couldn't breathe under the weight of it. I remembered when I was a kid, how big he had seemed back then, how scary.

"You fucking little ingrate," he said calmly. "You're not doing this on my dime. That doctor's gonna march back in here, and you're gonna tell him you've calmed the fuck down. Do I make myself clear?"

I shrank under his stare. I could feel myself doing it, even though I didn't want to. He was my father. If I told the doctor I was a boy, I could go home as one. But I had to face Dad at the end of the day. He had the power to make my life a living hell.

Then I thought: it was already a living hell.

Dr. Jacobs was back. "Any updates?" he asked.

"She'll have the surgery," Dad said. "The testicle, the penis, all of it. Just get rid of it."

No, I thought, panicking. No, they couldn't do this to me. He couldn't do this to me. I felt my heart picking up speed until it actually hurt. Sweat beaded on my skin, drenching me. The hospital gown stuck to my skin. The heart monitor to my right blared so loudly, we all clamped our hands over our ears, except for the doctor, who didn't look fazed. I couldn't breathe. My vision went hazy and white.

♦♦♦

When I came to, Mom and Dad weren't in the room with me. Neither was Dr. Jacobs.

What if Mom and Dad had signed off on the surgery, and the doctor was getting ready for it at that very moment? I was scared—at least I thought I was. My feelings kept slipping away from me like water through a sieve. It was such a dull kind of fear that I had the suspicion somebody had sedated me. If only somebody would sedate my goddamn mother.

I had to do something. I didn't know what, but I had to do *something*. For whatever reason, I kept thinking back to that talk I'd had with Miss Marbury back in March, three months ago now. She saw me. Michelle saw me. My parents didn't see me. But that just meant I had to find the people who did and surround myself with them.

"You will keep silent," my ancestor warned.

But I just couldn't. Not anymore.

I pressed the *ASSIST* button on my bed. A young, friendly nurse darted swiftly into the room. I asked her if I could use the bathroom. She was kind enough to take the electrodes off my chest after shutting off the EKG machine so it wouldn't sound. I think she expected to keep watch over me, but a loud beep outside called her attention, and she left again after promising she'd be back.

If I didn't act now, I'd never get the chance again. I opened the locker behind my bed and put on the clothes Mom had left there for me, along with my phone and wallet. I used the adjoining bathroom for real, because I wasn't sure when I'd get the opportunity to next. While in there, I ripped the patient ID band off my wrist with my teeth. I spat it out in the sink.

And then I left. Nobody stopped me in the hallway. They probably thought I was just a visitor. I boarded the elevator and rode it down to the first floor, willing it to move faster. In the lobby, the walls were a sickly beige color, like imitation butter. A bunch of receptionists sat at the registration desk with dividers between them, taking patient info from visitors. I walked past them. I walked out the sliding doors and into the parking lot. I kept walking.

I ran. I had come out, ironically, on Ash Street. I couldn't help thinking it was a sign of some kind, that this was the start of the rest of my life. Apart from the hospital and a small bed-and-breakfast, Ash Street was a residential area, muddy-brown houses flanked with red doors. I knew that if I headed north, I'd hit Bridge Street. From there, I could loop back around to Essex. I just had to be fast.

The adrenaline lent me speed. On Essex Street, I jumped on board a trolley, taking it to the terminus at the far end. It let me off in front of the famous Witch House where Jonathan Corwin used to live. He and Samuel Sewall and John Hathorne were the three most prominent judges in the witch trials, sending twenty innocent people to their deaths. But unlike the others, Corwin never expressed regret for what he'd done. Instead, he died with the riches he'd seized from his victims' households. I looked up at the gray three-story mansion with its three brown roofs. A lace curtain moved in one of the tiny windows. Probably just a tourist peeking out at the town square. But I imagined it was the judge's specter watching over his legacy, making sure that nobody had come along to disturb it.

I sprinted south to Summer Street. Neither of my parents' cars was in the driveway. They were both still at the hospital, unaware of my escape. I took the spare key out from behind the transom light. With sweaty hands, I unlocked the door and let myself in.

Mom liked to keep black garbage bags in the front closet for trash collection day. I took one and bolted upstairs to my room. I tore clothes off my hangers and stuffed them in the bag. I grabbed some cash, my phone charger, and my birth control pills, which I normally kept hidden in an old pair of shoes. I was running low; I didn't know when I'd next get to buy some.

Last of all, I tossed some of my Skeletronics vinyls in the bag. In the event that I ran out of money, I was going to need something to sell. I had all the songs on my phone, anyway, and in my head, long memorized. It was a constant concert going on in my brain.

Salem's commuter rail station was on Bridge Street. From the outside, it didn't look like a train station—more like a library on a college campus. It was surrounded by a mix of trees that didn't belong together: short, bushy ones with full leaves and skinny, dark pines whose tops reached for the clouds. The depot on the inside was all chilly concrete and glass waiting rooms. I went to the purchase window and bought the first available ticket to Boston. Evie lived out there somewhere. I didn't know where. I didn't know at all whether she'd be pleased to see me, or if she'd agree to put me up for a while. Mom and Dad had cut her out of our lives so thoroughly, I didn't even have her phone number.

If our situations were reversed, I would have helped her. The only thing I could do was hope she shared the sentiment.

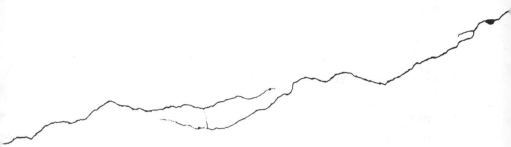

15

Boston's North Station looked the way I imagined an international airport must be. The tiled floor was so clean that I watched a guy drop his doughnut and pick it right back up. Or maybe he just didn't have standards. The ceiling with its glowing lights was held up by steel columns, not concrete like at our train station back home. All the trains went by the names of colors. From my platform, I watched the Orange Line disappear down a tunnel, an actual orange stripe painted down the side of the train's sleek chassis for easy identification.

I remembered something about Evie that I hoped would help me find her. In college, she had majored in software design, and shortly after graduating, she'd been hired by this big video game company in downtown Boston. It wouldn't have surprised me if she had been on *Salem Online*'s dev team. I felt my stomach clench at the thought of that game—the thought of Michelle. I couldn't bear picturing what she was going through right now.

Leaving the train station, I looked around but felt lost. I was in a neighborhood called the North End—which might as well have been the North End of London, because I had no clue where I was going. I stood in a narrow street between attached storefronts, American flags hanging out the windows. In the gaps between shops, I saw tall corporate buildings. I pulled up my phone and looked for a city map. Might as well take advantage of this technology while I could. It was only a matter of time before I got kicked off the family phone plan.

By sheer luck, the Financial District was just south of the North End. I legged it there, following Milk Street, but wound up lost again in a place called Post Office Square, a small, grassy park between high rises. I was beginning to realize how good I'd had it growing up in a small town. A college-aged girl stopped to talk to me when I asked her for directions. She knew the name of the gaming company right away; she told me what street she thought it was on.

I was getting tired just from walking. I wondered how much of it was the sedatives' doing and how much of it was that weird thing where my hormones were trying to kill me. I stopped at a street vendor to buy a bag of salty onion curls.

Downtown, I found the most random shit mystifying—like the standing aluminum mailboxes on the corners, and the people who dropped actual mail inside. The architecture here was old in a way that Salem's wasn't. Salem's was old because it offered a glimpse into seventeenth-century America, pristinely preserved by the nutsos who had inherited it. Some of Boston, it seemed, tried to compete with Europe itself, Gothic Revival and Victorian behemoths ripping off the Old World edifices of Vienna and who knew where else. If you'd asked me to pick Boston out of a photograph lineup, I didn't think I could have done it. There was something about big cities, with their sprawling, nonsensical layouts and unmitigated verve—no room for residences? Just build on top of the shit you already have!—that made them all look the same to me at a glance.

By the time I finished my snack, I'd found Evie's workplace. I looked up the length of the steel corporate building, unnerved by the height of it. The building didn't belong to the gaming company alone; they inhabited the fourth floor. I rode the elevator up to a lobby with carrot-orange chairs for visitors, blue and white hexagons on the wall.

"Can I help you?" asked the receptionist, who didn't bother getting up from his desk seat.

I told him I was looking for Evie Bishop but didn't know where she lived. He remembered her immediately.

"Evelyn Bishop? Nice girl. Hasn't worked here in about a year and a half."

A sense of dread overtook me. I might have been lost in Boston for real. "Don't you have an address for her on file?"

"Well, yes," the guy said, frowning. "But for privacy reasons, I—"

"I'm her brother!" I burst out.

He looked at my chest, though he quickly averted his eyes. I remembered too late that my hair was long and my tits had swollen to an A cup.

"Just call her," I begged. "Or text her. Please? Tell her Ashley ran away from home. She'll understand, I promise."

It must have been the desperation in my voice that convinced him to pick up his phone. I collapsed heavily into one of the orange chairs. The full weight of my exhaustion settled around me, and before I knew it, I was dozing off.

Out of nowhere, I was being shaken awake, my entire vision filled with Evie's face.

"What the hell happened to you?"

If I could only pick two words to describe my sister, they'd have to be *mousy* and *butch*. Maybe that didn't make sense, but anyone who saw her would have picked the same words. Evie's hair was long, straight, and unstyled. Her big round eyeglasses would have put a librarian's to shame. She had powerful shoulders, broad arms and legs, and a thick neck. Despite all that, she was shorter than me. And she always looked like a deer in headlights, because she blinked too much in the course of conversation. Sometimes she even stood around with her mouth open, forgetting to close it.

"Ash," Evie repeated. "What happened to you?"

I came back to myself, to the feeling of her broad hands on my shoulders, securing me. I really thought I might cry. "Got my period a year ago," I mumbled.

Evie's eyes roamed around, blinking way too fast just like I remembered. She slowly released me, looking over me again. "Mom did this."

"Wasn't just her," I said.

I told her everything. I told her about getting my period on the soccer field and all my teammates seeing it. I told her about the visit with Dr. Tran, getting bullied out of school, Mom's insistence that trying to be a girl would be easier for me in the long run. I told her about the salt wasting. The only thing I didn't tell her about was Michelle. If I started talking about Michelle, I wouldn't know where to stop.

Evie felt my forehead with the back of her hand. I didn't blame her for thinking I sounded like I had a fever.

"You'll come home with me," she decided. "Get some rest. You look like you're about to collapse."

"Don't send me back to them," I begged.

Evie shook her head. "I wouldn't send you back to a place I narrowly escaped myself."

◆◆◆

I zoned out on the car ride to Evie's place. I didn't remember getting inside the apartment, or the conversation that must have followed. I slept dreamlessly, filled with fleeting impressions that I was safe.

When I woke up, I was in a spacious room with bare brick walls, facing a giant window. I climbed off the bed—which I took to be Evie's—and drew close to the glass, looking outside. The assortment of buildings looked cold and gray and busy. I went downstairs into the main apartment, realizing I had been sleeping in some kind of closed loft. The floor was hardwood and echo-y.

"Aw, Sleeping Beauty's awake."

Trina Herrera was Evie's longtime girlfriend, a super-slim girl with a massive curtain of heavy black curls. Her hair was the first thing you noticed about her, like some medieval countess's trailing train. She was wearing a bright yellow tube top today, her belly button exposed. There was a puckered scar on her left cheek where, I remembered learning, one of her sisters had punched her during a family reunion while wearing an engagement ring.

"Where's Evie?" I asked.

"In the kitchen. She'll be done in a few minutes." Trina sat down on the couch and reached for the remote to a sleek TV. "Want to watch something?"

"Nah," I said, heading for the kitchen.

Evie was arguing heatedly with somebody over the phone.

"Yes, he's here, Mom." Pause. "What are you talking about? When did I ever—" Pause. "No, I'm not sending him back to you! And stop calling him she!"

She hung up, sat down on a stool at the island, and gestured for me to come over. "Mom and Dad are pissed," she said.

"Pissed they can't control me, you mean."

"I guess. She said she might send the police after you."

My stomach dropped. "Can she do that?"

"I don't know," Evie said. "I have a hard time seeing the cops hauling ass out here to pick up a seventeen-year-old who's visiting his sister for the summer."

"Why does Mom even care?" I asked. "She obviously hates me. Why does she want to bring me back?"

Evie shook her head. "She's wrong about everything, but I don't think she hates you. I think she thinks she's doing you a favor, in her own twisted way. She was right about one thing, though. We can't let you go untreated if you have salt wasting."

"They can't cut off my dick, Evie! Please—"

"Who said anything about that? We'll just take you to get those shots you need. The salt ones."

"But don't I need my parents with me for that?"

"Not if it's a medical emergency, which I'd say this is."

Evie's girlfriend invited herself into the kitchen. She sidled around the counter, leaning against Evie's shoulder. Her eyeshadow was very dark, big hoops jangling in her ears.

"He looks like a girl," Trina said, the queen of sensitivity.

"Yeah," Evie said, scratching her chin. "Can you do something about that?"

Trina sat me down at the island, wrapping a towel around my neck. She fetched a pair of scissors—I'd forgotten she was a hairdresser—and spent the next twenty minutes snipping at my hair. The cool, flat metal of the blades tickled my ears. When she took the towel away, I felt cold air on the back of my neck. Tell you the truth, I'd forgotten what that felt like. Dark brown locks littered the floor in feathers. She gave me a hand mirror and let me look at myself in it.

It was me. It was a style far shorter than anything I'd ever worn, but I could see myself again, the high contours of my face, the sharpness of my jaw. And then I couldn't, because tears were biting at my eyes, and I was shaking.

"Shh, mijo," Trina said. "We got you now, baby boy."

I was so grateful to her that I didn't complain about being called a baby.

16

I woke up in a state of disorientation, confused about where I was and how I'd gotten there. It came back to me when I sat up, felt the blanket bunching around my waist, and saw the brick walls of Evie's apartment. I was on the couch in her living room. I was in Boston. I was safe.

Safe for now, anyway. I sat up straighter, reaching for the garbage bag full of my belongings on the floor. I heard footsteps, and then Evie dropped down in the armchair on my left.

"Took off from work for a few days," she said. "Told them it was a family emergency."

This qualified as one, if anything did.

"Right," she said, like we were continuing a conversation I wasn't aware of. "We'll go get you fitted with a binder today."

"A what?"

She glanced at my chest with an awkward little nod. "Take care of that problem."

It had never occurred to me that anything could be done to flatten my chest short of actual surgery—which I still would have liked, but which was obviously off the table right now. That led me to another thought. "I wish I could get the ovary taken out. Dr. Tran wouldn't agree to it because she said I might change my mind later, whatever that means."

"It means people are obsessed with women's reproductive systems, so even though you're not one, they want you to keep it. They figure it's their business what you do with your body as long as you have one." Evie shifted impatiently in her chair, like she'd had this conversation tons of times and was sick of it. "Don't worry about that right now. You have your birth control. You can probably get the ovary taken out when you're eighteen."

"Why are you being so cool about this?" I asked.

Evie made a rueful noise deep in her throat. "I still remember the day they brought you home from the hospital," Evie said. "Mom kept crying and crying because they couldn't tell what sex you were. She acted like she was the one being punished, like it was her life that was about to get harder. Dad insisted that you had a penis, so that meant you were a boy; he was the one who put 'male' on your birth certificate. And of course, by the time you were four years old, all you wanted to do was play with Tonka trucks and eat worms. I realize that doesn't always mean anything, but a lot of the time it means something. And instead of seeing that as something positive— her kid getting to be himself—Mom sort of just seemed resigned to it."

She paused, blinking even more rapidly than usual.

"I don't know about you, but to me, when I was growing up, Mom always seemed like the better parent. Or the lesser of two evils, anyway. She'd get disappointed instead of angry. Instead of violence, she'd use emotional manipulation. She was the one I'd try to get through to, try to convince . . . but it's exhausting, trying to convince your own mother that you're human. I wouldn't wish that on anyone else."

I absorbed all this in silence, not sure what to say. "And honestly?" she went on. "It could've been me, Ash. I could've been born with CAH; I had the same odds as you. Have you done Punnett squares in bio class?"

"Sure," I said.

"Then you should know how this works, but I'll remind you. Being intersex is autosomal recessive, or at least the kind you have is. That means both Mom and Dad have a recessive copy of the allele. If you graph it out on a Punnett square—"

"There was a one in four chance they'd have a kid who's intersex."

"Right. Or you can put it this way and say that there's a 25 percent chance any kid they had would be born intersex. Those are the odds we were dealing with."

It all came down to a damn coin toss. It was wild how genes worked. It wasn't just that Mom and Dad had to meet at the right place and the right time for me to be born; *their* parents had to do the same. Because at least one of Mom's parents and one of Dad's parents had to have had that recessive gene.

"But with odds like that, how come I'm the only one in our whole family who ended up actually being intersex?"

Evie went quiet for a moment, then said, "I don't think you were. Grandma said as much. Mom's mom. When you were still little."

"Said what?"

"I overheard her talking to Grandpa one Christmas. She said of course Mom would have a kid like you; she couldn't escape it. Just like they couldn't with their kids."

I felt more alert than I had all week. "Are you saying Mom's got an intersex sibling?"

"Not for sure, but that's what it sounded like."

"You think Mom knew? Growing up?"

"I hope not," Evie said.

"Why?"

"Because I don't want to think that she knows how hard this is, and still has no empathy for you. It's easier to not hate her if she's just being ignorant."

I didn't know what to think or feel. This was an awful lot of information to pack into the span of a few days.

A yawning Trina trudged into the living room, but left soon after for work. After breakfast, Evie and I took the elevator down to her lobby, where a freaking door attendant stood inside the revolving door, wishing us a good day. I hadn't even registered him when I first got here. I was glad to see Evie had done well for herself.

We went out past the underground parking lot and walked west until we hit a shopping district called Downtown Crossing. Whole food markets and outdoor clothing racks dominated the brick street. A couple of storefronts were totally boarded up. GameSpot and Sprint stood across the narrow way from each other, glowing signs glaring as though they couldn't believe the audacity of their competitor. The street reminded me of Essex Street back home, because there was nowhere for cars to go. But instead of dark houses and dark trees for landmarks, we were surrounded by skyscrapers that grew no smaller and drew no nearer, no matter how long we walked.

Evie led me inside a small, nondescript store that was so dimly lit, I wondered at first if they hadn't opened yet. Thongs were hanging off of hooks on the walls, embarrassing me. I turned and walked straight into a display rack stacked with dildos.

"Evie, what the hell?"

"Shh," she said, though it looked like no one else was here. "This is the only brick-and-mortar store around here that sells binders. You want to get one online and find out it's the wrong size?"

"He just needs a binder," Evie told the spiky-haired woman behind the counter. "Can you measure him?"

"Sure thing," said the lady without so much as blinking. She took out a tape measure, which I eyed warily. "It's okay, hon. I just need to get your size."

She told me to lift my shirt, then measured the area around the bra I was wearing. The tape felt cold against my bare skin. The lady handed me what basically looked like an ultra-tight wifebeater in a plastic package. I asked her where the dressing room was so I could try it on.

"At the back, next to the restroom." She gestured at the package. "You need to step into it like you do a dress."

"A dress?" I asked.

"Put it inside out and upside down. Step into it—not the armholes—pull it up to your belly button. Grab the sleeves, pull them up, and put your arms through them. Et voila."

It sounded kind of daunting, but I went in the dressing room and did as I was told. That thing was tight as hell. It felt like wearing a sports bra that just happened to be a size too small. I pulled my shirt back on over it and walked outside. I wasn't at all sure it had worked, since I had been afraid to look in the mirror and find out that it hadn't. But the clerk started clapping. Evie gave me a thumbs-up.

"Take it off every eight hours," the lady said. "And don't sleep with it on. You should be good to go."

When we were outside the store, I couldn't stop poking myself in the chest. It felt flat again, like it was supposed to.

"Evie! Look at this!"

"Cut that out," Evie said. "You look like you're molesting yourself."

We stopped in a couple more stores for errands Evie had to run. There were no words to describe how good I felt while we were shopping, which ordinarily wasn't my favorite hobby. If I happened to meet a stranger's eye, I knew he or she wasn't seeing a girl, but me. It felt like I had been in a coma for a whole year, had woken up, and was relearning the world.

Around lunchtime, we went to Summer Street—Boston had one too—and entered the South Station subway. On the train, I surveyed the people we were riding with. One woman in a feather boa held a marionette on her lap. She stroked it as if it were a child, whispering in its ear. Another guy yelled "Praise Jesus!" every time we passed through a tunnel.

And here I'd spent my whole life thinking people in Salem were weird.

Evie and I got off the train in a neighborhood called the West End. It didn't look any different from the rest of the city, at least to me, but Evie gave me a history lesson.

"This place shouldn't exist," Evie said. "It used to be a working-class neighborhood of immigrants. Jews, Syrians, Greeks, and Italians, mostly. Sometime in the '50s, Boston Urban Renewal decided they wanted to remove those elements. So they razed it to the ground and displaced everybody, put up all this fancy real estate for urban transplants, and called it a day. A few years ago, the mayor issued a formal apology. But it's already too late; what's left of the community is scattered."

That made me feel kind of sad, even when we visited a bright and airy café with retro tables. We both ordered clam chowder—New England style, duh.

"You know," I said. I felt embarrassed, but I had to get this out. "Thank you."

Evie shrugged, sipping her cola. I think she was embarrassed too.

"So you had to go for a whole school year as a girl," she said.

"Yeah," I said. "Well, no. I lasted at Lawson until January."

"Your friends turn on you?"

I nodded, but then I thought about Michelle.

"What?"

"I . . . I have a girlfriend. Or had."

"Nice," Evie said.

"Not nice. Her parents totally freaked out, and now she's at some conversion camp in Indiana."

Evie sighed. "Poor kid."

"If I went down there," I said, "you think I could break her out?"

"No, I think you could get in trouble for trying. Depends on the state, Ash. It might sound shitty, but her parents are allowed to send her wherever they want."

"But she'll get hurt in that place!" I protested.

Evie looked uncomfortable. "I know."

"And we can't do *anything*?" I balled my hand on the table, afraid I'd punch something.

"Best thing you can do is find out if she has any other family who'd be willing to take her in," Evie said. "Then you can write to them to let them know what happened."

That made me think of something else. "You said you wouldn't send me back to Mom and Dad . . ."

"I won't," Evie said. "You'll stay with us, long as you can."

"How long is that?"

"I don't know," Evie said. "But I know if we try to send you to school here come September, we're going to run into some trouble, because I'm not your legal guardian."

"What if Mom agreed to let me go?"

"You really think she'd do that?"

I thought of the bag of makeup she'd given me for Christmas. I was forced to concede that she probably wouldn't.

"We'll think of something," Evie said.

♠♠♠

That night, Evie put a sleeping bag in the room she used as an office. She pushed the computer table up against the wall, emptied out her filing cabinets, and said I could use them to store my clothes.

"Give me a while," she said, "and we'll get a proper bed in here. Some drawers, maybe."

She was giving up her private work space for me. I wasn't so self-centered that I couldn't tell what a big deal that was. "Why are you so . . ."

"What?"

"Nothing," I said. I'd wanted to call her cool, but didn't want to embarrass her again.

Evie stopped in the doorway on her way out, looking me over. "You're happy," she said. "I can tell. Good."

She turned off the light and went outside. I listened to the city sounds outside the window: trash cans banging, trucks backing up, the rush of traffic like a gentle wind. This must be what happy felt like, after all. I had almost forgotten.

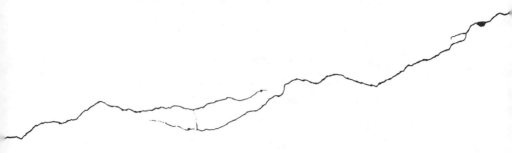

17

The next day, Evie and I visited the emergency room for my salt wasting meds. To my surprise, I was given an ID bracelet, too, printed up right there on-site. It looked like a dog tag, except it went around my wrist, not on my neck. *ADRENAL INSUFFI-CIENCY*, it said. *NEEDS STRESS DOSE CORTISONE*. I had to wear it at all times, which was creepy. But it was better than passing out and dying in the event that I couldn't administer the meds myself.

The doctor gave me a pack of disposable syringes and a couple of tiny bottles of what I guessed were the cortisol and other hormonal shots. He warned me not to go over the prescribed dosages—once a day and once every two weeks, respectively—or I could give myself liver damage. I told him not to worry. My dad drank like a fish and had never had any health problems. Superhuman livers probably ran in our family.

Evie took me home, where I spent some time figuring out how the needles worked. The pamphlet that came with the meds said to shoot myself in the thigh or the butt. I was sitting on the living room floor, rolling up my pants leg, when Trina stormed in like a tempest.

"That stupid pendeja!" she said—which I didn't know at the time was redundant. "If she changes my hours one more time—"

"Huh?" I asked.

She ignored me at first, digging around through the drawers beneath the coffee table. She slammed the drawers shut and sat down. "My boss is a bitch," she said.

"Sucks," I said. "Can't you just quit?"

"Oh, she'd like that, wouldn't she?" Trina said, like I was supposed to know. "Got a million girls lined up to do my job!"

I found out that day she was a little theatrical. After Trina left the apartment again around afternoon, Evie said she had somewhere she wanted to take me.

"It's called InterPersonal," she said. "The secretary said they meet for an hour once a week to reaffirm their solidarity."

"Sounds like a cult," I said.

"It's an intersex support group," Evie said. "Smart-ass."

"Support group?" I asked, wrinkling my face. "I don't need support."

"After the year you had?" Evie returned. "Just try it."

So at five o'clock that night, we took the train to the South End and got off on a street filled with Victorian townhouses, all attached in a neat, unending row. We walked to Washington Street, which looked just the same to me as all the other streets, except that at one point we passed underneath noisy, suspended train tracks, the Orange Line zipping above our heads. Finally we stopped in front of a large church whose facade looked gold in the descending sun. A single round, kaleidoscopic window hung above the double doors.

"You go in," Evie said. "Call me when it's over. I'll come pick you up."

"Wait, where are you going?" I asked.

"To the movies. You can't come. It's rated R."

I rolled my eyes but went inside the church. There were people sitting in the pews, about a dozen of them, but they were all talking and goofing off. I felt nervous about approaching them, and that wasn't normal for me. Barring extenuating circumstances, like my mom shoving me into a skirt, I tended to feel pretty confident about myself.

I was saved from having to do or say anything when a head turned my way. Its owner stood up and said, "What are you staring at? Get out."

They were too far away for me to see them clearly; as far as churches went, this was a big one. "I'm not staring!" I yelled across the aisle.

"Well, get over here, then," they snapped.

I skirted around the giant, trickling baptismal font in the middle of the aisle. If you asked me, there had to be a better place to put that thing. When I drew in view of my accoster, I wasn't sure whether I was looking at a man or a woman. They were still standing; they were tall—much taller than me—and white, maybe twenty years old. They had the face of a classical beauty, framed by a heavy jaw; a flat torso; toned arms; and a prominent Adam's apple. Their legs were skinny, their hips round. Their hair was a mess of frizz pulled back in a messy bun and covered with a kerchief.

"Oh," they said—and their voice was ambiguous, too, somewhere between "boy whose balls just dropped" and "chain-smoking old lady." They managed to look disappointed in me before I'd even done anything. "You're just a little kid."

"Uh, I'm seventeen," I said.

"Whatever," they said and sat down.

"Bishop?" asked a bald Black guy in his thirties.

"Yeah," I said. I figured I'd better sit, so I slid into an empty pew.

"Welcome. I'm Ted. Anyway," the guy said, turning away from me, "reserving a spot is a long shot. That's why I thought I'd start tomorrow."

I had no idea what they were talking about, but I was afraid to interrupt and draw attention to myself, so I sat and listened.

"Just let me do it," said the kind of bitchy one from before. "If you don't follow up with them every day and annoy them until they cave, they're not gonna give us a spot. I'll handle it. You won't get anything done, and we'll still be talking about it this time next year."

"A real barbecue would be so nice," said a young white girl with a soft voice—and by young, I mean much younger than me; maybe twelve. She had waves of platinum hair and big brown eyes like a ragdoll's, fixed dreamily on the church ceiling.

"Are fireworks legal in Boston?" asked a guy my age, rocking a 'fro.

It took me a while to understand that they were discussing a potential Fourth of July celebration. They wanted to hold it in one of the public parks but apparently needed a permit for the space. I expected at some point that they would start talking about their bodies, their challenges, their dilemmas. But by the time the full hour and a half had passed, the most pressing issue anybody had brought up was that their parking meter was about to run out of time. What the hell was a parking meter?

I picked up a few names. The guy with the 'fro was Thomas. The bitchy one was Ariel—further complicating matters, because the name was unisex, just like mine. The little girl was also Ariel, an incredible coincidence, unless it had been chosen for similar reasons. But the other Ariel didn't like sharing their name, so the little girl had to go by Airy. But nobody really introduced themselves to me directly, much less asked me any questions.

I didn't know what I felt—relieved, maybe, that I hadn't had to talk about myself, but disappointed that I hadn't heard anybody else's stories. It would have given me some peace of mind to know I wasn't the only one mistreated over something

I had no control over. The reality was a little more mundane. Intersex people were just people. They worried about what they were going to eat for dinner and whether their mom would be on time to pick them up. I guess I should have known; I worried about all the same things.

When I was leaving the church, the little blond girl, Airy, caught up with me. I was on the bottom step out front, and she tugged on my wrist, then handed me a folded-up sheet of paper. I unfolded it to see a charcoal sketch of my own profile staring back at me. The detail was incredible. She must have been drawing during the meeting, but I hadn't seen her doing it.

She smiled at me. With a little wave of her charcoal-smudged hand, she hopped the rest of the way down the steps and ran to a red buggy parked down the street.

I decided I could at least come back for next week's meeting. Maybe it was the kind of thing that grew on you.

♠♠♠

"Ash," Evie shouted in the kitchen Sunday afternoon. "Phone call."

I had a feeling I knew who it was. I mean, it could really have been only a handful of people. I steeled myself and entered the kitchen, where Evie gave me a grim look. *What'd I tell you?*

I took the phone from her as she left with her mug of tea. "What?" I said.

"Ashley?" Mom said.

She was back to sounding meek and timid, like I was the one who had mistreated her for a year. Now that I'd nearly died, the guilt trip wasn't working.

"Ashley," Mom said. "When are you coming home?"

"I'm not," I said.

"You have to, baby," Mom wheedled. "I'm your mother. You live with *me*, not—not your sister."

"I wanna live with Evie now," I said.

"You're being silly," Mom said quietly. "You don't want to leave your hometown behind."

It was telling, I thought, that she knew the thing I'd miss most about Salem was Salem. Not her. It meant that on some level, she knew she had alienated me. Maybe it wasn't just ignorance, like Evie wanted it to be.

"Mom," I said, "did you know one of your siblings might be intersex too?"

She went silent for so long, I thought something had happened to our connection.

"Mom?"

"What do you mean, one of my siblings . . . ?"

"Evie said she found out when I was little. She heard it from Grandma."

"No," Mom said. "That's not true."

She was frustrating me already. "There are worse fucking things to be than intersex, Mom."

"There are boys, and there are girls," Mom said in a hollow voice. "You're one or the other. There's no in-between."

"But I'm in-between, Mom. So are you saying I'm nothing?"

Mom didn't reply.

"Forget it," I said and hung up.

Just when I thought nothing could make me feel shittier about myself, she always rose to the occasion.

◆◆◆

As much as talking to Mom had bothered me, it had put a couple of things into perspective for me too.

I was in-between. I was a guy, and nothing and nobody could change that. But if not my brain, my body, at least, was both male and female. If a body had a penis, then it was a male body. Right? But if a body had a vagina, it was a female body.

My body was both a male body and a female body. In being both, you might say that it was neither. Except neither meant nothing, and I wasn't nothing. I didn't believe that. Not anymore.

A lot of the problems I'd faced in the prior year had come about from people denying the half of me that was male. Had some of them come from my denying the half of me that was female?

It wasn't like I was about to run out and buy dresses and watch *RuPaul's Drag Race*, or whatever chicks did when they weren't having pillow fights in their underwear. But all this time, I'd kept fighting and fighting against my own body, and hating it, and wishing it would stop being what it was. Maybe I'd only hated it so much because of the way other people had reacted to it. When I looked back on my life, my having a vagina hadn't informed my childhood in any way. It had always just been this thing between my legs that I needed to make sure I cleaned in the shower. The dread I'd felt when it had started to bleed was because the guys I'd grown up with had seen it, and were making fun of it.

How many of the issues people had with their bodies were rooted in the unfair standards society put on them? You saw it a lot with overweight people undertaking these dangerous crash diets. Or with people getting plastic surgery. If only somebody out there had said "Some guys get their period" or "Some girls don't get their period," maybe it would have been a nonissue.

Suddenly I wondered: Just how many guys fell under the same category as me? In my family alone, there were very likely two intersex people. InterPersonal had fourteen members. Growing up, Mom and Dad and even doctors had led me to believe that I was so different, so impossibly rare, that I couldn't hope to meet other people going through what I was. In Boston, I'd met thirteen. And hadn't Miss Marbury given me a list of *several* intersex support groups that were based here? So InterPersonal wasn't even the only one.

When I went back to the group the next week, I found the courage to ask how there could be so many of us in one place.

Ariel, the bitchy one, raised their eyebrows at me. "What are you talking about? Are you laboring under the delusion that this is rare or something?"

"Well . . . yeah?"

"What percentage of the human population has red hair?"

I didn't know, and I said so.

"Two percent. Now what percentage of the population do you think is born with characteristics of both sexes?"

"I don't know . . ."

"Two percent. Sit on that one, honey."

I did. I was floored.

"No need to be rude, Ariel," said Ted. He shifted around. "Most hospitals have something called a gender committee. When a baby is born with ambiguous genitalia, the hospital assembles a team with an endocrinologist, a psychologist, an ethicist, and a member of the clergy. They discuss which gender they're going to assign to the baby. Then they perform the necessary surgeries to see it out."

"Surgeries?" I asked.

"Yeah," said Ariel. "You're saying you never had any surgeries?"

"Um . . . no. I mean yes, that *is* what I'm saying." Maybe because my parents had never really agreed about my gender;

when I was born, Dad had wanted me to be a guy, and Mom had hoped I'd be a girl.

Ariel gave me a distasteful look. "Lucky," they said. "The gender committee usually tries to make your body match whatever chromosomes you've got. But that doesn't always work out."

"Take Swyer syndrome, for instance," Ted said. "A person born with Swyer syndrome has XY chromosomes, like a typical perisex boy might. They have testicles, but they've also got a working uterus. They can carry a baby with no complications. So what do you do with that?"

"*And*," Ariel injected, "it's not all as simple as XX and XY. You can have as many as four chromosomes and as few as one. What do you do with *that*? You can't magically cut out chromosomes, or add more."

"So what if the gender committee gets it wrong?" I asked. And what was a member of the clergy doing telling doctors how to cut up babies?

"They get it wrong all the time," Ariel said.

"In fact," Ted said, "I'd argue there's no such thing as getting it right. Cosmetic surgery should never be performed without the patient's consent. Imagine if the law allowed parents to give their newborns facelifts and nose jobs. I was born with a blind vaginal pouch and undescended testes. The doctor pressured my parents into removing the testes and raising me as a girl. But nature won out, I suppose."

"I didn't even get that consideration," Ariel said glumly. "No committee, no nothing. The midwife said to my mom, 'It's a freak. Which do you want, a boy or a girl?' She chopped up the parts my mother didn't want like they were a salad. Now the old yenta doesn't even talk to me."

It had never occurred to me that I might actually be the

lucky one in some ways. The last year of my life sucked balls, but at least I got to live normally for the first sixteen.

"Which one are you?" I asked Ariel, kind of hoping to change the subject. "Boy or girl?"

"Both," Ariel said. "You little brat."

"They didn't do any of that with me," Thomas said. "They let me wait and decide for myself. What about you, Airy?"

Airy shrugged with a shy little smile.

"So, like, maybe people are coming around?" Thomas said.

"Maybe they are wherever you're from," I said. "Not in Salem, Massachusetts."

"Ash," Airy piped up. "I'm from Salem too."

"You are?" I asked. "What are you doing here?"

"We moved for Dad's work," she said. "I haven't been to Salem since I was nine." She giggled suddenly. "Are you a witch?" she asked.

"Yeah," I said. "The contemporary kind."

"What's that mean?" Airy asked.

"Means I'm talking out of my ass," I said. "Sorry—don't tell your parents I said that word."

❦ ❦ ❦

June 16 was Corey Dietrich's birthday. When we were friends, we used to celebrate it by going to a place called Dairy Witch Ice Cream, where we blew through our whole month's cash. Always we tried at least one of the more exotic flavors, like Grape-Nut custard, but in the end, I'd get the coffee-flavored soft serve, and he'd order the buttercrunch maple walnut sundae. No wonder he had such bad teeth.

This was the first of Corey's birthdays that I wasn't celebrating with him. Our friendship had cooled to a point where it didn't even make sense to consider him a friend anymore, but I didn't think it was right not to text him. I was in the living room with Evie and Trina, watching a movie, when I sneaked my cell phone out to send him a quick message. **happy bday**, it said, short and to the point.

I was surprised when he texted me back right away. **thanks man! where r u?**

with my sister, I replied. **staying with her for a while.**

whoa. ur in boston

yeah.

It was weird that he was being so talkative all of a sudden. **what's boston like?** he asked.

crowded and weird. i'm downtown.

whoa

you must be in a good mood.

My phone vibrated, alerting me that he was calling me. I took it in the kitchen so I wouldn't bother Evie and Trina.

"So," Corey said, "you're talking to me again?"

"What do you mean?" I asked, irritated. "You're the one who stopped talking to me."

"What?" he burst out. "No I'm not! After I apologized for—you know—Mom said I should back off and let you decide if you still wanted to be friends. But you never really asked me to hang out anymore, so . . ."

Was it really possible we'd both been waiting for the other to make contact? Just when I thought my life couldn't be any more confusing, nature found a way.

"Hey," Corey said. "Can we hang out? My mom takes the train to Boston every day, so we have one of those year-round passes. I could be there in half an hour. We could meet up somewhere."

"You wanna?" I asked skeptically.

"Come on, don't give me the third degree . . ."

An hour later, I went to the South Station to meet him. By the time I got there, with its exterior resembling an amphitheater, he was already standing outside—in that ridiculous pink sweater of his. Worse, he had fitted his head with a knit cap that kind of resembled a droopy sock. You'd think he would have been overheated in that getup, but Corey was the kind of guy who complained year-round of being cold. His mom said he'd broken the thermostat in their house once because he wouldn't stop cranking it up.

"Hey," he said when he spotted me. "You look like you again!"

"Yup," I said.

We decided to visit the Freedom Trail, where we'd had our field trip back in eighth grade. We argued for a moment about where it started, then mutually headed for Boston Common.

"I'm sorry again," Corey said. "For, like, everything that went wrong in school. I heard Jay Tulley beat you up in gym class."

"You think Jay Tulley could take me on alone?" I shook my head. "Had two other guys with him."

Corey's eyes went as wide as saucers. "Coward!"

"Forget about it," I said.

"There's, like, a bunch of stuff I wanted to ask you about, but since we stopped talking . . ."

We'd reached the park. The Freedom Trail started there, a cobbled street bordered by benches, umbrellas, and lampposts with round heads. They looked like skinny black Q-tips sticking out of the ground.

"Go ahead," I said. "Ask me anything."

"Okay," Corey said. "Can you get yourself pregnant?"

"Nope."

"Can you get somebody else pregnant?"

"Nope."

"Can somebody else get you pregnant?"

"Maybe."

"But you're a guy."

"Yup."

"I didn't know there were guys who could get pregnant," Corey said distantly. "Wow."

I stopped to buy him a wrapped ice cream sandwich from a food cart, though it wasn't anything like Dairy Witch Ice Cream. He made a mess of it the moment he tore it open. The hot sun probably didn't help; the melted vanilla ran down his fingers, the chocolate wafers turning to sludge.

"Corey," I said, suddenly inspired. Corey was a huge gossip in school. "Do you know anything about where Michelle is right now?"

Corey licked ice cream out of the crumpled wrapper. "What do you mean?"

"Her parents sent her to some camp in Indiana," I said. "I don't know what city."

"Oh, yeah, I heard about that!" Corey said. "A religious camp, right?"

"But do you know the city the camp's in, or when she left?" I asked. "Maybe she told you about it?"

"I'm sorry, man," Corey said. "I like her, don't get me wrong, but we mostly only hung out with each other because we had you in common."

I felt like I'd already exhausted all my leads. "She has other relatives in Massachusetts," I said. "They don't live in Salem, but they visit every Thanksgiving. Do you think your parents would know anything about them?"

Corey shook his head blankly. "Why's it so important?

She's a little old for summer camp, but she'll be back in September, right?"

"I don't know if she will," I said haltingly.

Corey was already distracted, trying to walk on the back of a bench like a tightrope. Of course he fell off of it, at which point, he complained. He was a bit oblivious like that. But he wouldn't have been Corey if he had been any other way. I'd known him since I was nine years old. I was surprised to realize how much I'd missed him.

♦♦♦

Evie's apartment had a balcony, something I'd only ever seen in luxury units before—so when I said she did well for herself, I meant she did really freaking well for herself. The night of Corey's birthday, after he had gone home, I went out on the balcony and sat on the wicker chair, enjoying the cool breeze and the waxing moon. It was stark and white tonight, almost blue actually. It reminded me of this book I'd read once, *The Moon Is a Harsh Mistress*, which had started off great but quickly derailed into being the author's political soapbox. Like, no, dude, I seriously didn't need to know that you viewed all women as simultaneously hypersexual and infantile and thought polygamy was rad because you wished you could bang three of them at once.

Trina came outside and dropped into the seat next to mine. She sighed in a sad way, which I took as my cue to ask her what was the matter.

"Quit my job," she said. "Don't tell Evie about it just yet. I don't wanna argue."

It was kind of an honor that she confided something in me before she told my sister. "Sure, I won't tell."

"Guess I'd better start looking for something else, huh?" Trina gave a defeated little laugh.

"You went to school with Evie, didn't you?" I asked. "You don't have to be a hairdresser if you don't want to, right?"

"Went to school, but never finished," she said. "I didn't have the mind for it. Not everybody does, you know. And that's a good thing. Can't have the world overrun with accountants and bankers. Who'll fix your carburetor?"

"Our robot servants, I bet."

"Oh yeah? Then they can do the accounting too."

"You saying you want to be a mechanic?"

"Nah. Not if it means I have to do anything to this glorious hair."

It was pretty glorious, I had to give her that.

"You ever think about having kids someday, mijo?" Trina asked.

The question caught me off guard. "Growing up," I said, "Mom and Dad told me I could never have them. So I got used to that. Never really questioned it."

"You never thought about marrying a girl and having babies with her?"

"Mostly I just thought about growing up and driving monster trucks." These days I thought it might be cooler to be an architect.

"You can't have kids," Trina said, "but that doesn't mean you can't have kids. You know? You can adopt. Or beg some pretty boy to inseminate your wife for you."

Gross. "You want to have kids someday?" I asked.

"We're gonna," Trina said, like that was that. "A girl named Zelda and a boy named Link."

"Dear God," I said.

"You think about getting married?" Trina asked.

I fell silent, trying to recall how I had considered marriage growing up. I must have assumed I'd do it, just because it was what most people did. It wasn't something I'd ever thought about at length. And I guess I assumed that fantasizing about weddings was something only girls did.

"I don't know," I said. "It was only pretty recently that I even started to think about being in love . . ."

I told Trina for the first time about Michelle. She didn't seem all that surprised when I got to the part about the Christian antigay camp, which made me wonder if Evie had told her already. I decided I didn't mind if she had.

"Humans are incredible," Trina said on a sardonic exhale. "Keep coming up with new and creative ways to hurt each other. You'd think after two hundred thousand years, they'd run out."

18

Evie had been trying to get me an appointment with a therapist ever since I showed up in Boston. I didn't think it was necessary, especially since she would have to pay for it out of pocket, but she kept saying that everyone could benefit from therapy. She finally got me into a forty-five-minute time slot with a guy named Mr. Sewall. He had sleek blond hair and icy blue eyes, and there was something about him that was cold and impersonal, but maybe that was better for me; an impartial opinion might be refreshing right now.

We sat down together in his small office, which somehow had room for about half a dozen different kinds of chairs.

"Tell me about your childhood, Ashley," Mr. Sewall said.

I felt the way Bridget Bishop must have felt when she was on trial, forced to plead her case before the judge.

"It was fine," I said. "Normal, I guess."

"Get on with your parents?"

I shifted in my chair. "I guess so."

Mr. Sewall asked how my relationship was with my dad growing up. I must have reacted badly, because the next thing I knew, he was asking how long I had been afraid of him.

"I'm not," I said instinctively. Then I thought that in the interest of getting Evie her money's worth out of this session, I should probably be truthful. "Since I was five, I guess.

I wanted to play with him when he was in the garage, but he didn't want me in there, so he hit me."

He didn't need to know about the part where I'd wet myself. That was personal.

We talked about a whole bunch of things I didn't think were related, like whether I'd ever had pets, and what my dream job was when I was in kindergarten.

Afterward, I told Evie, "That seemed pretty pointless."

She shrugged. "He might not be the right fit. It can take a while to find a therapist you click with."

"Well, I don't want you to have to keep shelling out hundreds of dollars per hour for trial and error," I said. "I'm good with InterPersonal for now."

She blinked a few times. "You sure? Seemed like you weren't that into it."

"It's growing on me."

◆◆◆

Ted Dixon from InterPersonal asked me if I'd like to go to something called the HarborWalk with him and a couple of other members. Thomas Demaine would be there, he said, and Ariel Sharev—the bitchy one, not Airy Teeling. Evie wouldn't be back from work for a couple of hours, but Trina said she thought it sounded fine, so I told him I would come.

He picked me up in his car and took us to a brick road alongside a weedy, cobbled one dotted with stone picnic tables. The twin roads wound around the blue-green bay, roped off with black chain links. The huge pier ahead of us was rust-colored and metal, built up like a cage on both sides. We passed a big building with arches that had to be a seafood restaurant, if the outdoor tables shielded by the brick roof were anything to go by.

"What's the point of this?" Ariel complained. "We just walk?"

"What's the matter," I said, "did you forget how?"

Parts of the road were incomplete, and we had to dart around swirly yellow construction signs. When the road picked up again, we were on a kind of bridge leading across the water. Thomas pointed out boats, cars, and fisheries like he'd never seen them before—which I guess was possible, since he'd moved here from landlocked Arizona. He took out his phone and snapped photos of a resting seagull.

It was kind of nice being near the water without any weeping willows to block the view. We stopped once for breaded fish sticks and onion rings. We watched a guy dressed like a mime juggling increasingly improbable amounts of balls. A sudden rainfall cut our excursion short, all of us dashing underneath the outdoor umbrellas for cover. When Ted dropped me off at home, it was about four o'clock. I just happened to get a text from Evie at the same time, saying I should come home right away.

My first instinct was to worry that something had happened to her or to Trina. I raced to the elevator and rode it up to their apartment.

There were police inside, two of them, a guy and a lady. The guy was standing with his hands on his hips, but neither one seemed to be doing much of anything. Trina was eyeing them like they were a fungus. The lady noticed me first.

"Hey, Ash," she said, like we were friends. "Got a call from your mother about you running away?"

I looked at Evie for a cue, but her face betrayed nothing.

"She's awful worried about you, Ash."

"Bullshit."

"Oy! Carajito!" That was Trina. "Don't talk to cops that way."

The cops didn't appear remotely bothered, though. And then I remembered something Evie had said nearly two weeks ago.

"I'm visiting my sister for the summer," I said. "How is that running away? My parents know where she lives and they know that I'm here. My mom's just being a basket case. That's kind of her thing."

"Are there problems going on at home, Ashley?" the lady cop asked. "You fighting with your mom?"

"Like you've never fought with your mom before?"

"All right," the guy cop said. "We'll let her know everything's fine here. But we can't keep getting calls from your mother. We're not babysitters, Ashley."

"Good," I said. "I don't need one."

They left without much fanfare. Trina closed and locked the door, leaning against it as if she would blockade it with her body. Her eyes were dark and stormy. "Well," she said. "This is bad."

"Why?" I asked. "They left."

"If Mom keeps calling them," said Evie, "they're going to get annoyed enough to do something about it. Like drag you home by the hair."

"My hair's too short for that."

"Jesus Christ, Ash. You always have a mouth like this?"

"I could never get away with talking to cops like that," Trina said. "Hell, my brother got a bullet to the knee just because he didn't move his car on time."

I felt kind of bad now.

And I couldn't help thinking that if I didn't find a way to make Mom stop, she'd have her way and force me to come home. She'd chop up the parts of me she didn't want—"like a salad," Ariel had said—and probably I'd wind up doing something drastic. It was possible that Bridget Bishop wouldn't be the only member of our family to die with a noose around her neck.

❧ ❧ ❧

It rained throughout the next day, which meant staying cooped up indoors. I figured I'd play some games on my phone, but when I slid past the lock screen, it said *Service Unavailable*. It took me a while to realize Mom had finally taken me off the family plan. She was trying to get me to come home by holding my phone hostage.

"Forget it," Evie said. "I've got a prepaid you can borrow. We'll port your old number over. Only I'm not going out and buying minutes in this weather. You can have it tomorrow."

"Thanks," I said. Then I thought of something. "Could I borrow the house phone right now?"

"What for?"

"I think I want to call Aunt Delilah."

Aunt Delilah was Mom's younger sister. She lived in Florida. Normally I only ever saw her on Thanksgiving. She was the friendliest of Mom's siblings, so I thought I would begin my intersex inquiry by talking with her. I wanted to know which of our aunts or uncle was like me. I couldn't explain it, but having that knowledge would make me feel like less of an outsider in my own family.

Evie agreed to let me borrow the phone in the kitchen. I grabbed a seat at the island and cradled the phone against my shoulder, listening to it while it rang.

"HELLO?" boomed Aunt Delilah's voice on the other end. I held the earpiece a few inches away from my ear. I always managed to forget how loud she was.

"Hi, Aunt Delilah," I said. "It's—"

"OH MY GOD, ASH! HI! HOW ARE YOU DOING, SWEETIE?"

"Aunt Delilah," I said. "I don't really know how else to put this. Do you know that I'm intersex?"

"Inter-what, sweetie?"

"I was born with a penis and a vagina."

"Ash!" she said sternly. "Those aren't very polite words!"

How could they not be polite words? They were literally medical terms.

"Anyway," Aunt Delilah said, "are you sure that's even possible? One of your little school friends isn't playing a prank on you, is he?"

Not only was Aunt Delilah probably not intersex, but Mom had never told her that I was, either. Had she told anyone, besides the people who would've seen me every day, out of necessity? Would she never have gotten around to it? I tried to picture what this year's Thanksgiving might have looked like, me sitting at the table with inexplicably long hair, maybe even forced to wear a skirt—the elephant in the room.

"Aunt D," I said, "do you have Uncle Henry's and Uncle Christopher's phone numbers?"

Aunt Delilah gave me my uncles' contact information, but I didn't feel like calling them just then. I hung up with her, processing what I'd learned. If one of my uncles was intersex, their parents had never told the rest of their siblings about it. No wonder Mom had thought I must be wrong. And there was something else that dawned on me, complicating matters. What if my grandparents had had an operation done on their intersex child—like Ariel's mother had—but had never told them about it? Then the person I was looking for might not even know that he or she was intersex . . . in which case, there was a possibility I'd never find them.

On Saturday night, I had a bad dream about Michelle. She was standing in a crowd, the bystanders gawking at her. I couldn't reach her; there were too many of us, maybe about fifty. It was nighttime. Somebody picked up a torch and lowered it to the ground until the flame spread. The fire passed over my feet but didn't hurt me. It crawled toward Michelle, who seemed to have frozen. She screamed. I didn't know if she got hurt, because at that moment, somebody handed me a baby and asked me to look after it. Not that that had anything to do with the rest of the dream. Dreams were weird, especially mine.

The bad feeling stayed with me Sunday morning. I'd woken up early, about seven, and it was raining again. The sky outside the window of Evie's office was so gray and murky that little light reached into the room. I got up and went out to the living room, rubbing my face, trying to wake up. I had to do something. I had to get Michelle out of that prison.

But I was powerless. The only other time I'd felt this powerless was when people were telling me how to dress and who to be.

If I'd wanted somebody to tell me how to live my life, I would have gone to church on Sundays, I thought. If it wasn't for church, Michelle wouldn't even be in this mess. As far as I was aware, there were no secular movements to abolish people's right to love whomever they wanted. Just religious ones.

My thoughts melted together into a sad, confusing slush. All at once, they ironed themselves out.

If I was going to have any chance of getting Michelle home, I needed help from the inside.

I ran around the apartment, looking for a pen and some paper so I could leave Evie a note. I must've been louder than

I'd thought, because Trina came into the living room in her Big Bird pajamas, yawning. She asked me why I was awake at this hour.

"I'm going to Lynn," I said. "I have to go to church."

"Aw, you found Jesus."

"Do you think it's okay for me to go to a Black church? I mean, will people feel weird with me there?" I didn't know the protocol for any of this.

"Dunno," Trina said. "They might be wary, considering that white boys occasionally go around shooting them up. Tell you what, I'll go with you. Anyone gets uncomfortable, I'll take you out of there fast."

"That would be amazing. Thanks."

We got dressed, ate breakfast, and took umbrellas with us when we left for the train station. Trina dozed off on the train, though I didn't know how she managed it, because the guy sitting across from us had a wildly barking Chihuahua in a tote bag. I shook her awake at the Lynn stop. When we got off the train, it was still overcast. We walked the couple of blocks to the address I'd looked up online, the hissing rain making puddles on the uneven ground.

We found the church without any trouble. Inside, the parishioners were dressed fancy, in sequin dresses and snazzy hats. Trina and I sat down, and I started awkwardly trying to make eye contact with people.

One little old lady to the left of us sat staring hard at Trina, like she was worried that she was hallucinating. "Excuse me, ma'am," I said. "I'm wondering—um—I'm a friend of Michelle Carrier . . ."

"You just missed her, then, didn't you?" the lady said. "That whole family went on vacation to Florida."

So that was the official story. "Do they have any family

156

who stayed behind? Or do you know how I can contact one of her uncles?"

She frowned. "Afraid I can't help you, young man."

Just then, the service started. On the whole, it involved a lot more singing and clapping than ours did. It seemed like the parishioners were actually encouraged to talk back to the preacher when he said something they liked. There was none of the solemnity of Salem First Church, which made me think that, in general, it was a happier place to be.

Afterward, Trina and I stood under the awning just outside the front doors. The rain had slowed down, turning thin and misty. I approached a few other people to ask about Michelle's relatives, with no success.

"You should've told me you were looking for your little girlfriend," Trina said.

"Lot of good it did me," I muttered. These people were being pretty mum about the Carriers' whereabouts. I didn't know what else I could possibly do for Michelle. I felt like a failure of a boyfriend.

"Ash," Trina said. "I just had a brilliant idea. I think I'll come work here!"

"Here?" I asked skeptically. "In Lynn?"

"Why not?" Trina said. "People make longer commutes every day. I'll find someplace between here and Salem that's hiring. How many hairdressers you think there are in Salem who know how to do Black hair?"

"That's great for you, I guess," I said.

"Great for both of us," Trina said. "I'll tell you why. You know when people do most of their gossiping? When they're sitting in the salon chair with nothing else to do. You give me a couple months, tops. I'll find somebody who knows your girl."

I really hoped she was right.

♦♦♦

I found out from Ted at InterPersonal that Boston held an enormous Fourth of July celebration every year. The festivities were apparently pretty intense. First, at nine in the morning, City Hall Plaza was going to host an official flag raising. After that the parade would begin, making its way to the Granary Burial Ground to lay wreaths on the graves of Paul Revere and John Hancock. Along the way, there were going to be live musicians and historical reenactments, including a face-off between colonists and British soldiers. The Fourth of July, I took it, was to Boston what Halloween was to Salem.

"I tried hard to get us a spot in the parade," Ted explained during our session. "But organizers turned us away."

"What do you mean?" I asked. "Why?"

"Something about how made-up groups aren't allowed in the parade, or they'd have to let everybody else in too."

"That makes no sense," I said, angry now. "Aren't all groups 'made up' by definition? And being intersex isn't made up! Should I go down to city hall and drop my drawers for them?"

"Do that, and I'm pretty sure they'll ban us from future parades too."

We couldn't march in the parade, or have a barbecue onsite, but we could still watch the festivities. Ted promised to text me when he and the other InterPersonal people found a spot to gather. Meanwhile, Evie and Trina and I headed out to the Charles River Esplanade, a park in the Back Bay where a stage shaped like a conch shell had been constructed. The Boston Pops Orchestra was going to perform during the fireworks.

I watched families unfolding their picnic blankets. One guy dressed in full American Revolution gear tossed a Frisbee to a redcoat. We had come early, but Evie said we had to, or there would be no room.

"Hey. What's up?"

Uncle Henry was in town for the holiday weekend. I was lucky he'd agreed to meet up with me after we'd talked on the phone. I'd had no luck getting ahold of Uncle Christopher, and I was tired of leaving vague voice mails for him, so I was really hoping Uncle Henry would have the information I was looking for.

He was a short guy with graying auburn hair and a face lined with exhaustion. I knew from holidays past that he was pretty irritable, but once you got a few drinks in him, he became everybody's best friend. Case in point: He looked annoyed when he had to sit down on the picnic blanket with us, until Trina passed him a bottle of something labeled Applejack. The relief was palpable on his face.

We got to talking about the circumstances of my birth, the real reason I'd asked to see him.

"I always knew you were a hermaphrodite," Uncle Henry said after a couple of mouthfuls. The alcohol didn't just make him friendlier; it loosened his tongue. "Nicole made me swear not to tell anyone." He suddenly looked crestfallen. "Was I not supposed to tell you?"

"Uh, I kind of already knew," I said. I didn't like the word *hermaphrodite*, though.

"She told me the day you were born," Uncle Henry said. "Even before she told Jim."

"Really? Wow."

"She thought it was her fault, that she'd done something wrong and you were born that way as a consequence. She was scared about what your father would think. She wanted the doctors to hurry up and operate on you before he got to the hospital, so he'd never find out."

"Why didn't they, then? Operate, I mean?"

"I talked her out of it."

"*You* did?"

Uncle Henry's face reddened with drink. "Well, sure— she wanted to cut off your penis. Why should they do that? Huh? Tell me, why do women hate men so much? They'd cas- trate all of us if they could. There's something evil and sick about them."

I instantly felt disappointed. He hadn't stood up for me because he was thinking about my future and my rights over my own body. He'd stood up for me because he'd thought I might turn out to be a guy, which was somehow a more valuable thing to be than a girl. My dad had clearly felt the same way.

"Uncle Henry," I said. "Are you intersex too?"

The splotches on his face got redder with anger. "What? How dare you say that about me? I'm a full man!"

He stood up, unbuckling his belt as he got ready to prove it. A little kid sitting in front of us turned around, saw him, and pointed with a gasp. "Whoa, whoa, whoa!" shouted Evie, as Trina yelled even more choice words and a police officer hustled toward us.

I took that as my cue to leave.

As I edged away from Uncle Henry, I checked my phone and saw a message from Ted, with a location pin showing me where the InterPersonal group was camped out. They weren't that far away. Perfect timing.

❧ ❧ ❧

The next day, right after Evie had finished putting a bed in her office for me, the cops showed up at her apartment again. Trina wasn't home; it was just the two of us.

I was expecting the visit to be like the last one; I'd argue with the cops a bit, they'd go away, we'd put on the TV and veg out. I was shocked when one of them started handcuffing Evie.

"What are you doing?" I yelled. "She hasn't done anything wrong!"

Both of the cops ignored me. The one restraining her told Evie that she was being charged with "concealing or harboring a child."

I followed them all the way to the elevator. The cop who wasn't leading Evie turned to face me. "Well, Ashley," she said, "time to go home."

"I'm just going to run away again," I said quietly. It was eerie how calm I felt. "Keep dragging me back there if you want. I'll keep running away."

The cop reached for my hand. I jerked it back. Her face hardened.

"You want to be cuffed too?" she asked.

"Do it," I said.

She did it. I mean, I literally told her to, so in some capacity, it was my fault. I didn't care. Evie had done nothing wrong by taking me in. I'd done nothing wrong by running away. I knew who I was. I knew how I deserved to be treated. There was nobody on the planet who deserved to be harmed just because their identity didn't fit into one of two square boxes.

19

"All right, Ash," Officer Hollander said as she pulled up along-side my parents' driveway. I would have liked to throw the door open and run for it, but cop cars, I learned that day, didn't open from the inside. And anyway, I was still handcuffed.

"I don't want to have to bring you back here again," Officer Hollander said.

Being back in Salem made me think of the things I used to love about it, the things that could be enriching, even though they could be harrowing too. I thought of its history. When I was little, hanging out in my dad's museum, browsing the yel-lowed documents behind the glass, I found out that the young-est witch trial victim, Dorcas Good, was only four years old when she was put behind bars. Four years old. Can you believe that? The judges said that because her mother was a suspected witch, Dorcas must be one too. Wickedness was considered genetic, passed down from mother to child.

It seemed to me that Salem had a track record of cuffing its children to keep them silent. It was easier than having to sit down and figure out what was really the matter with them.

I was stony and silent when Officer Hollander got out of the car, came around to my side, and opened the door. Getting out of a car with your hands behind your back was a surpris-ingly difficult feat. I managed it at last; she shut the door.

Mom was waiting at the front door, her hands clasped in front of her white face. I'd never hated her before. Looking at her just then, I felt that I hated her.

Officer Hollander put her hand on my shoulder and walked me up the front steps to the porch. She unfastened the shackles around my wrist. I heard them pop open with a creak and a snap. "Your daughter's in lockup, pending bail," she told Mom.

"Thank you, officer," Mom squeaked.

I channeled the full force of my hatred into my stare and felt Mom shrink under its intensity. Did that make her feel proud? Having her own daughter arrested for being kind to her son?

We both stood and watched as Officer Hollander got in her car and drove away. Finally, Mom turned around to walk inside through the open door.

What did she think I would do? I bolted down the street and kept running.

I could hear her shouting my name until I was halfway down the block. She might have chased me part of the way; I didn't know. But she couldn't hope to keep up with my longer strides.

When I'd started running, it was without a plan in mind. But the moment I felt the air pushing through my lungs, straining against my chest, I knew where I could go.

I ran all the way north to Winter Street, pacing myself so I wouldn't collapse.

Miss Marbury lived on the same block as Parris Academy. I knew because she'd given me her contact information back when she was trying to help me out. I didn't want to burden her with my presence, but I needed somewhere to hide while I got in touch with Trina.

I found her house, which had a peculiar outdoor staircase

that wound from the first floor to the second. To me that seemed like a safety hazard, unless she had a really good alarm system. I rang her doorbell, the sweat cooling on my skin with the downwind breeze. She opened the door a few moments later.

"Ashley?" She sounded shocked. I realized she'd only ever seen me when I was presenting as female.

"My parents are trying to make me a girl," I burst out. "They made me do it for a year. I can't go back to them. I can't."

She let me inside her house. The doorway opened up on a kitchen, not a foyer, making me think whoever built it had been drunk. At least two pots and a kettle were sitting on the stove, all steaming. I was reminded of a train's thick white smokestacks. She led me underneath a staircase to a small sitting room with a threadbare throw rug. Her fireplace had one of those glass doors covering it when it wasn't in use. We sat down together at the table while I gave her the short version of recent events.

"The police made you come back here?" Miss Marbury asked, her face soft with concern.

"Why does everyone else's opinion of me matter more than mine?" I asked. I'd been wondering this for a while now.

Her smile faltered. "Can I ask you something personal?"

"What is it?"

"On your birth certificate," she said. "Does it say male or female?"

"It says male. How come?"

"If we can get you a copy," she said, "maybe it would put a stop to what your parents are doing to you."

"Why do we need an official document?" I asked, a little frustrated. "Why doesn't my word matter in any of this?"

Miss Marbury looked like she might cry. She blinked, and

it was gone. I knew then that she wasn't doing what my mother always did and making the situation about her. She was upset because I was upset.

"It doesn't matter," Miss Marbury said, "because we still live by a system that considers the convenience of the parents before the well-being of the child. Until that changes, kids in your position have to deal with a lot of hardships."

She helped me print out some forms from the Massachusetts vital records website, then left me alone to fill them out.

When I was mostly done, I went to find Miss Marbury in her back garden, where she was trimming some plants she called ballerina orchids. The flowers really did look like little dancers with pink bodies and white skirts, delicate arms poised over their heads. I thought of Michelle and swallowed over the tightness in my throat.

"All set," I say. "Except I need to give them an address to send the copy. And I don't really know where I'll be when they mail it."

"You're welcome to use my address," Miss Marbury said, wiping her forehead with the back of her hand. "I'll be happy to forward it to you."

"That would be great. Thanks."

She beamed at me. "Meanwhile, why don't we get you something to eat?"

"That's okay," I said, embarrassed. "I just need to text somebody. Then I'll be out of your hair."

"You're not a bother," Miss Marbury said, standing up.

There was dirt on her shoes and on her trowel, which she gently laid down on the flower bed. I thought that I might really like to hug her. Too bad the prospect was embarrassing. She seemed to know some of what I was thinking, anyway. She gave me a soft smile, rabbit-y on her sheeplike face.

I owed so much to so many people. If not for their generosity, I wouldn't have stood a chance in a world like this. I was a living testament to other people's kindness. I swear to God the good ones outnumbered the bad ten to one. Could I really have thought I was a monstrosity not that long ago? Now I understood that I was the luckiest person I knew.

♦♦♦

It turned out that I didn't have to text Trina because she'd texted me first—several times. Evie's bail had been a laughingly low $500, and Trina had already paid it. She was home now, but awaiting a trial date. The crime she'd been charged with was a misdemeanor. If she did get found guilty, it was a year in jail. Which seemed incredibly unfair given that she'd done nothing wrong. I was the one who'd run away and wound up on her doorstep. If anyone ought to be punished, it was me.

don't come straight back to our place, Trina texted. **this is probably the first place they'll come looking for you. get one of your friends from the support group to take you in for a day or two.**

Who could I bum with for a couple of days? Airy and Thomas were out of the question; they were kids themselves. I tried Ted, but he said he was out of the city and wouldn't be back until next Sunday. Tonight's meeting was called off for that very reason.

I quickly exhausted my list of contacts, except for Ariel. I didn't think they'd take me, and I didn't much want them to. But I had no other choice.

Fine, they texted me. **I'll be at Boston North in half an hour. Don't keep me waiting.**

I felt like a fugitive—and when I thought about it, I

supposed I was. I had to keep moving, keep running, unless I wanted to get snapped up and thrown back into the boiling pot. I made my way to the train station as quickly as I could, hoping that Mom hadn't called the cops again. If she had, I hoped the delay I'd created by staying at Miss Marbury's house meant I'd missed them.

When I stepped off the Newburyport/Rockport Line, Ariel was waiting for me on the busy platform, looking irritated as usual. I headed over to say hello, but they didn't give me a chance to get a word out.

"You sleep on the couch," they said. "Don't touch any of my stuff. Don't spend longer than five minutes in the bathroom."

"I bet you have loads of friends, don't you?"

I thought we'd leave the station, but instead, we walked to a different platform, where we waited for the Green Line. Ariel said they lived in the West End. Another train ride later, they took me to a sand-colored building with a red top, a few stories tall. The double glass doors were arch-shaped, red with a green frame. THE WEST END MUSEUM, read the sign above them.

"You live at a museum?" I asked dubiously. I couldn't help thinking of my father.

"I live upstairs from the museum, stupid."

They had a small apartment on the third floor. It was extremely cluttered; my mom would have thrown a fit just at the sight of the place. No fewer than four cats were prowling around on the hardwood, occasionally bumping into potted plants. Off to one side were a coffee table, a sewing machine, and a drafty window with a dish towel shoved through the crack. Ariel made me take my shoes off and leave them by the front door. They did the same. They locked up and went around gathering up items that were in their way.

"Here," they said, thrusting a pair of wrinkled pajamas at me. I unfolded them, curious to see what the shirt said. "*Intersexy?*" I read, incredulous.

"You wear that or you wear nothing," Ariel said sweetly. "And if you wear nothing, I'll have to gouge my eyes out."

They showed me where the bathroom was so I could get changed. When I came back out, they had changed, too, into a T-shirt and boxers. Why couldn't I have worn that? Jerk.

"Thanks," I said. "I know this is last minute and all."

"Well," they said with a poisonous smile, "just remember you owe me a big favor in the future."

I rolled my eyes. "Sure."

"You want something to drink?" Ariel was kneeling at the coffee table but stood up. "How old are you again?"

"Twenty-one," I lied.

"Bullshit," they said, disappearing in their kitchen.

They came back and we sat on the cushions at the coffee table, drinking chocolate milk. A tiny gray cat brushed against my ankle. I scratched behind his ear. I said, "Isn't this the neighborhood where all the original residents were kicked out?"

Ariel put their chipped cup on a coaster. "That's right. My parents were among them. My mother lives out on Portland Street these days."

But they'd said they didn't talk to her. I decided not to ask about their relationship.

"Almost no one can afford to live out here anymore," Ariel mused, leaning back in their seat. "I work at this museum, so that's different. But it was a weird upbringing, that's for sure."

"How do you mean?"

"We West Enders move around a lot. Itinerants, basically. Some might say refugees. And forget about keeping up with the friends you've made over the years. They're busy moving too."

"Sounds lonely," I remarked.

"At least I never kept up with anyone long enough to have to explain to them why I started virilizing so late."

"Virilizing?" I asked. "Like, becoming more masculine?"

"That's what virilizing means, isn't it?" they said, like I was a moron.

"I did the opposite," I said. "I was always masculine, but a year ago, I got my period."

Ariel flicked their eyes at my chest, not bothering to hide their smirk. "I noticed."

I'd taken off my binder for the night.

"I have 5-alpha reductase deficiency," Ariel said. "It's a different kind of intersex from yours."

"I never knew there were different kinds. Before I met you guys, I thought we all had the same condition."

"You'd know if you bothered listening when people other than you talked." I rolled my eyes again, though in the back of my mind I wondered if I seemed just as obnoxious and standoffish to Ariel as they did to me. "Mine's not inherited, like yours is. It's a random mutation, or at least I think it is. I have fully functioning testes, but they're on the inside. On the outside, I used to have both—a dick and a vag."

Their condition kind of sounded like the total opposite of mine. "Could I ask you something?"

"You're going to anyway. Just make it fast."

"What were you raised as? A boy or a girl? Because you said your mom . . . chopped you up."

Ariel peered bitterly into their cup. "She wanted a boy. My labia got cut off and my vagina was sewn shut—badly; I've had hundreds of infections over the years. Nearly died of sepsis once."

"I'm so sorry, Ariel." I really meant it.

"Sorry?" they asked. "Or glad you escaped the same fate?"

"Can't it be both?"

There was a long pause before they spoke again. "I'll tell you something. Not a day goes by that I don't feel angry at everything I've lost. I don't just mean the surgery."

"What do you mean, then?"

"I mean I can't get close to anyone. How could I? Just think about what a disaster dating would be. I like men. All right, so that rules out straight men, because I don't have a vagina. But gay men are ruled out, too, because . . . well, look at me."

"I think you're pretty."

"That's my point, genius."

"Just trying to help."

"I'm both a boy and a girl," Ariel said. "How could I ever find anyone who accepts me the way I am? Unless he were intersex too."

"I've got a girlfriend," I said. "She's not intersex, but she accepts me."

Ariel snorted. "She's probably a little bisexual."

"Maybe people are people," I said, "and all the labels we come up with for each other are a weird symptom of a shared OCD."

"Maybe."

"But I mean, there you go. Start dating bi guys."

Ariel laughed, then sighed. "Still . . ."

"What?"

"The thing I want most," they said, "my biggest, most hidden secret, is something I could never have had, even if they hadn't cut me into pieces."

I was afraid to ask. "What's that?"

"A baby," they said, resigned. "I could have one with a woman, ironically, though I'd need fertility treatments to do it. But I could never carry one myself. I could never feel my baby growing inside of me. I don't know why I wish that I could. It's not that I'm 100 percent female. If they'd cut off my penis instead, I'd be just as upset as I am right now."

Ariel looked at me fully for the first time. Their eyes were bright with passion and anger and still that same dull, sad, sick resignation. Their cheeks were brushed with light freckles I hadn't noticed before.

They said, "I don't hate my body. But sometimes I hate that God decided I wasn't good enough for a regular one."

20

I stayed at Ariel's place for a few more days. We discovered a shared love of Tommy Wiseau's *The Room*, aka the best movie ever made. For a couple of nights, we took to shouting "You're not my fucking mother!" at each other whenever we disagreed about something. We tried playing Scrabble, but Ariel was a cheater. They kept playing words that didn't make sense, like *gorn* and *flavorite*.

"What are you talking about? Gorn is when a movie is so gory, it warps back around and becomes porn. And flavorite is obviously a portmanteau for your favorite ice cream flavor."

"Sounds fake, but all right."

A text from Trina tipped me off that Mom had called the cops about me again. They knew that I belonged to InterPersonal, and they were sniffing around the other members' residences for me.

"That means they'll eventually check if you're here," Ariel said. "You'd better leave while you can."

"You think it's safe for me to go back to my sister's yet?"

"Should be. They'll probably have checked there already. What are the odds they bother checking there again?"

I dressed in the clothes I had first worn to Ariel's place. Ariel had washed them for me, even though they hadn't had to. When I was stepping into my shoes, I hesitated.

"Are you gonna be okay?" I asked. "If they come here looking for me?"

"Why wouldn't I be? I'll say you were here for a few days, but you didn't tell me you were a runaway. I'll say you talked about going to Indiana."

I'd told them a little bit about Michelle over the past few nights.

"Ariel," I said. "Thanks."

"Just get out of here before I change my mind and turn you in."

Now that I'd realized the bitchiness was how their species showed affection, I didn't mind so much. I felt kind of honored to be the recipient of it.

◆ ◆ ◆

I took the train to the Financial District, massively paranoid that at any moment, I'd turn around and find police tailing me. That didn't happen. I sneaked into Evie's apartment building, rode the elevator up to her floor, and let myself into the apartment. Both Evie and Trina were at work, but it felt amazing to be back.

Evie came home around four. When she saw me, she took two big strides toward me and pulled me into a crushing hug. I was surprised at how good it felt, how I melted against her, even as I thought it was kind of embarrassing.

She let me go. "Harboring a child," she said. "My ass."

"I guess they'd rather you kicked me out on the street."

She blinked owlishly at me a couple of times, which I understood was just her way of gathering her thoughts. "My trial date's in August."

"Is Mom seriously going to make you go through this?"

"We'll find out in August, won't we?"

Trina came home an hour later. She jumped on my back and gave me a noogie. Ow.

"Guess what, guess what, guess what?" she said, sliding off. "Got a little surprise for you, mi vida."

"New England clam chowder?" I asked.

"Better," she said. "Found somebody who knows your little girlfriend."

My heart started racing a mile a minute. I had to restrain myself to keep from throwing my arms around her. "Are you kidding me?"

"Knows her uncle, more like. Real hot and heavy for him every time he comes to town. See what I mean? Everybody trusts their hairdresser with their secrets."

"Did she give you his number?"

"No, but he's going to be in Salem two days from now. Does some consulting for a used car lot there. You could catch him then."

"I don't know that Ash should keep going back and forth when the cops are looking for him," Evie said.

"You don't? Me, I think it's the perfect way to make sure they never know where to look."

"I'm just saying, if they're waiting at the train stations, they'll catch him."

"Why would they be waiting at the train stations? He's not a serial killer."

"Listen," I said. "This isn't about me right now. I'm going to meet with Michelle's uncle and see if I can convince him to help her. If I get caught again, I'll figure something out, okay? You guys don't have to worry."

Evie's face was blank, though I knew her well enough to tell she was worried. Trina patted me on the shoulder, nodding.

It felt amazing to have people who cared about me without conditionals. Maybe it was because they'd too often been in the same boat. Some people would say they shouldn't love each other just because of their genital configuration. Well, if those people had known more people like me, they would have realized what idiocy they were promoting. If we were only allowed to love people who were the exact opposite sex of us, then who was I allowed to love? Nobody? That hardly seemed fair.

❦❦❦

I wasn't worried about getting caught by cops. But I was a little tired of traveling back and forth between Salem and Boston so often. It was bewildering to me that some people did this every day for the sake of their livelihood.

I trudged out to Lynde Street, between the rows of apartment complexes that didn't belong in Salem, half of them unfinished, scaffolding and girders leaning against them and running atop them. I followed the road to Gallows Hill with its ancient locust tree. For years, locals had maintained that this tree was the one where the accused witches had been hanged. Then a few years ago, some archaeologists came to Salem and argued that the hangings really happened on the other side of the hill. To this day, there were arguments about which location was accurate. But I didn't see how it mattered. It was a difference of a few feet at most.

I climbed up Gallows Hill, careful of the sliding black dirt. I skirted around the locust tree, but I didn't want to touch it, a rare moment of superstition for me. Carefully, I picked my way down the other side of the hill, stopping on a shelf of shallow soil we called Proctor's Ledge. In the past, the victims hanging here would have looked out and seen the old town square, their accusers' faces, maybe some stocks and pillories. Now the hill overlooked nothing more majestic than a Walmart.

Once down the hill, I followed the back of the Walmart to the used car lot. Faded yellow and orange flags whipped from the tops of the fences in the hot wind. A woman in a bright pink bikini was standing among the cars with her hands on her hips, a bored expression on her tan face. I wanted to think most men weren't dense and hormonal enough to buy something just because a sexy, half-naked chick was promoting it. But I should have known better. Already I saw a car salesperson homing in on a young guy who couldn't stop ogling her.

I went inside the building, which was surprisingly cold. It was so big and so empty in there that I felt it must have been a repurposed warehouse. I approached the secretary and asked her if Deacon Carrier was in today. She said she'd page him for me, and a minute or two later he was walking over to me to say hello.

I didn't know how I'd missed it before. He and Michelle's father were obviously twins. Their faces were identical, but instead of a satanic goatee, Michelle's uncle wore a full beard.

"Hang on," he said. "I think I've seen you before. You're . . ."

"Michelle's friend, Ash."

"That's right! She had such a crush on you when y'all were little."

So it really must have been obvious, and I was just an idiot.

"You're not here to buy a car, are you?" Mr. Carrier asked with a dopey smile.

"No," I said. "Actually, can we talk about Michelle? Do you have some time?"

He looked at his wristwatch. "If you can wait twenty minutes, I'll have plenty of time."

I told him I didn't mind. I went back outside to chat with

the lady in the skimpy swimsuit. She was a student at Salem State University. She wanted to be a dentist.

Mr. Carrier came out and found me before long. We went into a chilly cafeteria with a broken clock on the wall. He bought me a tuna sandwich, which I thought was really nice of him.

"You're not here for Michelle, are you?" Mr. Carrier asked. "She's in Florida right now. Joel says they're cutting back on technology for the summer. Petting some dolphins or something."

"They're not in Florida, Mr. Carrier," I said. "They're in Indiana."

He looked up from his folding chair. "Why'd he tell me they're in Florida?"

"Probably because he didn't want you to know they've taken Michelle to one of those antigay camps."

His eyebrows climbed toward his broad forehead. "That girl ain't gay."

Would it matter if she was? But I didn't say that, in case Mr. Carrier really did think it mattered. I wanted Michelle to have an ally right now, and I wasn't going to do anything to hurt her chances.

"Michelle's my girlfriend," I said. "We started going out in March."

"Wow!" he said. "Well, about time."

"I don't know," I said. "Her parents are really mad about it. That's why they sent her to Indiana."

"I'm not following."

I pushed away my half-eaten sandwich. I'd rather have not needed to say this, but it looked like I was going to. "It's because I'm intersex."

"Inter . . . what do you mean?" Mr. Carrier said slowly. "Are you saying you're a transsexual?"

"No," I said, letting his word choice slide. "I have congenital adrenal hyperplasia. I'm a guy, but I was born with both genitalia."

"Both? You mean . . . Is that possible?"

I was starting to understand why so few people knew intersex was a thing. Explaining it over and over again was exhausting.

"I don't think that matters right now, Mr. Carrier. Michelle's being punished unfairly."

"You want me to talk to her father about it?"

I didn't know how to say this without coming off as pushy. "I don't know if he'd listen if all you did was talk to him."

"What are you saying? If he doesn't listen, there's nothing I can do. That's his child."

"That's your niece," I said. "And she's amazing. Isn't she, Mr. Carrier? Isn't she the kindest, funniest person you've ever met?"

He folded his hands on the table. "She is very kind," he conceded.

"Then why does she deserve to be hurt, Mr. Carrier? She'd do anything to help one of us if we were in trouble. I know she's helped me so many times. What's it going to feel like when she gets out of that place, knowing at least one of us could have helped her, but everybody she loved let her down? If I were her, I'd never trust people again."

He looked like he was scared, somehow. He had been in the middle of picking up his canned soda to drink it, but set it back down.

"I'll have a talk with Joel," he said.

"But—"

"And if he doesn't let her out of there, I'll have to walk in and let her out myself. Nice coincidence, our being twins."

I couldn't be sure he really meant it. He could have just been saying what I wanted to hear to send me away. Or maybe, in the moment, he felt impassioned for Michelle's cause, but once I was gone, he'd find inactivity easier, like most people did.

But at least there was a chance he would follow through. There was a chance now. And as much as I hated it, a chance was the best I could do. It seemed a poor way to repay the girl who had sneaked me into Planned Parenthood, helped me hide my growing chest, and covered for me when I egged our principal's car.

※ ※ ※

"Hey, Ash," Thomas said as we were leaving the latest InterPersonal meeting. "Want to come over to my place? I don't really know anybody in this town. We just moved here from Tucson. I've got video games."

It had been so long since I'd hung out with a guy my age that I found myself jumping at the chance. "Sure," I said, then caught myself. "Let me ask my sister."

I texted Evie, and she said it was all right, as long as I was back by ten. Thomas gave me a little fist bump. We walked down the block, passing gated entranceways with sealed cellar doors.

"What'd you move here from Tucson for?" I asked.

"Nothing fancy," Thomas said. "My dad met this woman online, and they're in love now, and he thought we'd move here and she could move in with us. My mom and my dad are divorced. I've always lived with Dad, but you know, Mom still sends me video games all the time."

"Cool. What are we going to play?"

"I've got a ton, you can see what looks good to you. Or, actually, have you heard of this game called *Salem Online*?"

"You're joking." I couldn't keep the grin off my face.

"Nope. Really, I'm not! I thought of you right away. It's this murder mystery game where you either play as the good guy or play as the bad guy."

"I've heard of it. I mean, I've played it before."

"Cool, then you can teach me, because I tried a game last night and got executed, and then everybody was mad at me afterward. I don't know what I did wrong."

"Did you forget to claim a role on the stand? Or show the town your last will?"

"You're supposed to do that?"

Thomas's building was drab and gray, with a basketball hoop out front. We went upstairs to his apartment and I tripped over the cardboard boxes littering the floor. Thomas said he and his dad were still unpacking. I didn't think his dad was home, because the place was quiet and dark. He walked around flipping lights on. We went to his room, where a two-liter bottle of lime soda stood proudly on the floor. Clothes hung over the back of his computer chair. He tossed them on the bed and let me sit on the chair. Then he pulled over a stepladder and sat on that.

"Okay," I said as he booted up his PC. "First things first. You have any tokens?"

"Tokens?"

"You buy them in the game and they increase your odds of getting a certain role. Let's buy you some Detective tokens so you can start with something easy."

"Wow, I must really sound like a big noob right now."

"Sure, but what's it matter? Everyone starts somewhere, and no one wins all the time. Some people just like to forget that."

We visited the in-game shop to get him some tokens and some cosmetic items. Thomas leaned back on the stepladder.

He stretched his arms, yawning, and then pulled his shirt off and scratched himself. He tossed the shirt on the floor. He was wearing a sports bra and didn't seem to think anything of it. He saw me looking and shrugged sheepishly.

"Dad's always telling me not to go around in my underwear," he said. "But it's hot in here. And it's not even a dry heat like back home."

"Sorry," I said. "I just . . . forgot for a second."

"What? You mean, that I'm intersex? But we just talked about all that."

"Yeah, but I'm not generally comfortable about . . . you know. Letting it all out."

He faced me with a puzzled frown. "Why not?"

"What do you mean, why not? You get it, don't you?"

Thomas shook his head.

Where did I even begin, then? "My parents like to make me feel like there's something wrong with me. And when my classmates found out, I got bullied pretty hard. That never happened for you?"

"I don't think so," Thomas said slowly. "I mean, I've always known I was intersex, just like I've always known my mom's my mom, and my dad's my dad, and my name is Thomas."

"But nobody ever gave you crap about it?"

I was so distracted that I'd forgotten about the game. I think he had too.

"Well, no," Thomas said. "I know that maybe that's unusual. But my dad always told me, 'Some people are one thing or another, but you're in between. You can bring both worlds together. That makes you special, and you should be proud.'"

I held my hands on my lap. I felt bad about it, but I was seriously jealous. "You never looked at your body and hated it, or felt afraid of it?"

"No. I think it's awesome! I get to wear bras and stuff, but I don't have to buy tampons because I don't have, you know, those parts. And I look like a guy, don't I?" I nodded. "But if I committed a crime or something, and the police got my DNA, it would look like a girl's DNA, so they'd never be able to prove it was me."

"Whoa," I said, laughing. "I think I need a lawyer for this conversation."

"I'm just messing around."

"Yeah, me too." I couldn't even remember the last time I'd joked around with someone. I finally clicked around on his computer some, just to give the illusion that we were still paying attention to the game.

Nobody else in Thomas's family was intersex, and they still treated him like he was normal. But my family probably had at least one other intersex person in it, and nobody had reached out to me, or told me that I was born the way I was supposed to be. For the first time since all of this had started, I didn't feel scared or angry or embarrassed. I only felt sad.

Thomas sat there in his bra and his boxers, female from the waist up, male from the waist down, complete and at peace. "Listen, Ash. It's not an accident, our being like this. We were supposed to be born this way. You'll see it. I'm still working on Ariel, and now I'll work on you, and before you know it, you'll start to believe it for yourself."

I swallowed a lump of emotion. "Thanks, man," I said.

And then I changed the subject, uncomfortable, as I always was, with my own feelings. "You should pick a funny nickname for the game," I said. "You know, they randomize the names, but sometimes you get to choose. I like to go with Mister Fister."

"Nice! I'll be Dixie Normus!"

◈◈◈

Evie's court date was on the first Wednesday in August. I wanted to go along to show her my support, but she said it wasn't a good idea. My being there might fan the flames. Mom seemed to have called the cops off on me for now—maybe she was embarrassed at her inability to keep one kid in check, never mind two—but if I showed up in court, and so did she, the authorities might feel they were obligated to do something about sending me home.

So I didn't get to go with Evie and instead went for a long walk to clear my thoughts. My imagination allowed me to picture all kinds of terrible outcomes for her. If she had to go to prison for a whole year, what might happen to her? At least she'd be in lockup with other women. But I knew from experience that girls could be just as nasty as boys could. And you had only to look at Evie to know that she was a lesbian, as awful and stereotypical as that sounds. She'd be singled out in ways far worse than I had been.

It was kind of messed up that our prison system was more punitive than rehabilitative in nature. No wonder the rest of the world had less crime than we did.

Lost in thought, I walked out so far that I emerged in a neighborhood I'd never been to before. It was sandwiched between Boston Common and the West End. When I looked up, I had the feeling that I had walked right out of my world and emerged in some other realm. I was standing on a cobblestone street, a real one, not the imitation kind that you see so often in Massachusetts. There was an easy way to tell the difference. Fake cobblestone was a modern invention: a smooth imitation rock called a "sett." Real cobblestone was rough, bumpy, and discolored in grays and yellows and blues, mossy where rain had accumulated over the years. To make it, the colonists had dug up the soil beneath their feet, found it loaded with these weird rocks, and reshaped it, having few other building materials at their disposal.

The street underneath me was narrow, an alley really, bound by the backs of old brick houses—colonial flags in their back doors and ambitious vines growing up the siding. It sloped so steeply downward that if I hadn't been paying attention, I might have tumbled right down the road and fallen on my head. And when I looked between the houses, I saw the most impossible sight of all: real lampposts, the kinds that needed to be lit every night and extinguished the next morning by a lamplighter with a hook.

Standing at the top of that slope, I thought anyone would have felt the way I did: like if I dared to walk the rest of the way down, I'd come out the other end of a time machine and run into Paul Revere. And it was so quiet in that alley, so peaceful, that I held my breath and heard birds chirping. Where were the birds even hiding? There weren't any trees out this way.

I took out Evie's prepaid phone, snapped a picture of the street, and sent it to Ariel. **yo, where's this? i'm in your neck of the woods.**

They were at work, so they didn't reply for a few minutes. **Acorn Street. Why are you stalking me?**

I crouched down and touched the bumpy, colorful rocks, closing my eyes, imagining all the people who must have passed over them in the last four centuries. Hard to believe, but it came down to luck that I got to pass over them too. If Mom and Dad had never met, I never would have been born. Or if Mom had had an amnio done when she was pregnant, if she'd known during embryonic development that I was intersex, she could have aborted me and gone on to have another baby, one whose body was more to her liking.

Understanding dawned on me. Why had I never realized

the obvious before? If Grandma knew she had the CAH gene but didn't tell any of her kids, she might have had amnios done on all of them when they were still in the womb. Prenatal testing would have told her which one of them was intersex. And from there, for a woman with the right prejudices, the next step was obvious. I could see it happening just as clearly as if I'd been there on that day.

The intersex aunt or uncle I was looking for didn't exist anymore.

◆◆◆

I went back to Evie's place late in the afternoon. She was already there. She paused Netflix, and I rushed to sit next to her on the couch, to ask her how the trial had gone.

"We're meeting again mid-August," she said.

"What? Why?" It was frustrating that they were drawing things out like this.

"Mom and Dad were there," Evie said. "They want the charges changed from harboring a minor to kidnapping."

Kidnapping. The word hung between us, ludicrous yet haunting.

"It's not kidnapping if I ran away," I said.

"I know."

"Let me tell them that," I insisted.

"No. Ash—"

"Just once. Okay? Please? Let me go to the next trial date. Ask your lawyer if it's okay. I want to tell them what you've done for me. I want to tell them what our parents tried to do to me. Please?"

She looked weary, but she promised, "I'll ask her if that's okay."

"You helped me so much," I said. "I wanna help you."

She put her hand on my shoulder. She unpaused Netflix, but I don't think either one of us was paying attention to the show.

"Just remembered," Evie said. "Something came in the mail for you today."

She handed me a sealed envelope with my name on it. I tore it open.

Two pieces of paper fell out. The first was a handwritten note.

Dear Ash,

Remember that form you filled out at my house? I don't know if we're going to see you again in the autumn, but I hope this helps you, wherever you go.

Thinking of you,
Miss Marbury

The second paper was a copy of my birth certificate. It listed the hospital I'd been born in—North Shore Medical Center—and both of my parents. It had the seal of the State of Massachusetts stamped across the bottom. But what really caught my eye was the gender field.

Sex: Male.

I pressed that paper against my chest with trembling fingers. Nothing and nobody could tell me otherwise now.

21

The Edward W. Brooke Courthouse was the weirdest building I'd ever laid eyes on. It was made of what I thought was limestone, each individual brick perfectly sized, cut, and wedged in place, with a roof of gray shingles. It was five stories and shaped like a clothing iron. Whoever had erected it had placed it on the street corner at a slant, so if you were coming at it from the sidewalk, you'd have to go around the side to get through the door. The weird angle, as well as the size of the thing, made the edge of the roof look like a pointy needle pricking the sky. You might have expected the people walking in there for a day's work to be astronauts instead of lawyers.

It was a spaceship on the outside, but a shopping mall on the inside. I stepped into a huge, echoing white hall with scattered vending machines. Staircases with golden railings ran along the walls, each floor with its own catwalk, so you could theoretically stick your head out of a courtroom on the fourth floor and shout below to somebody on the first. Some of the floors had benches for people to sit on while they stopped and took a break. The only thing it was missing, I thought, was a water fountain for kids to toss coins in. Anybody coming to this place to make a wish had to be pretty desperate.

I hoped I was dressed okay. I'd worn black slacks and a white button-up, even though it was hot out. I didn't want to look like I wasn't taking Evie's situation seriously. Trina was wearing a yellow sundress. She linked her arm through mine and led me up the stairs to the third floor, where we went into a courtroom of sunny blond wood that frankly looked more like a conference room than a place where people's fates were decided every day.

Mom and Dad were sitting at one end of the long, oval table. I didn't look either of them in the eye. I sat down with Trina as close to Evie as the lawyers would allow.

The judge came in and shook hands with everybody, introducing himself as Judge Tsang. He was slender and gray-haired and seemed cordial enough, though he looked as though he would have preferred to be outside enjoying the sun, which meant all of us were in the same boat.

"I see we have here the minor in question," the judge said, turning to me.

I wasn't sure if I was allowed to talk yet. But this seemed like a much more lax environment than the kind that was always being shown on TV. Maybe it was that way because Evie was only being charged with a misdemeanor.

"Now, Ashley," said Judge Tsang, and I was cringing already, because he was using the kind of voice you use with babies. "Today we're holding a best interests hearing, which means we're going to ask you how you feel about your family. I'm of the opinion you should have been brought in here much earlier. Why are you so upset with your parents?"

What did he mean, much earlier? There was only one other court date before this one. Anyway, if he didn't know by now why I'd run away, then Mom and Dad must have withheld some key details about this case. Well, I was about to blow their cover.

"They want to cut off my dick," I said.

Trina coughed.

"Your . . . ah, you mean your penis," said Judge Tsang.

"That's what I said."

"I'm sure you don't really believe that, Ashley."

"No? Why don't you ask them?"

I turned in my seat and tossed a dirty look at Dad, the piece of shit. I'd never felt confident enough before to do that. It felt good, even if he returned it with much more skill.

Somebody who must be my parents' lawyer said, "Ashley is intersex, Your Honor. She and her parents have been arguing over her gender presentation. She began menstruating last year."

"Yeah, well, I don't do it anymore," I cut in.

Evie's lawyer, a young woman with a southern accent, leaned over to whisper to me that I might want to tone down the interruptions.

"Intersex," the judge said. "Is that a medical term?"

Was he fucking serious? I realized he was a legal professional, not a doctor. But how could we have a judicial system that was totally blind to 2 percent of its own population? How could it govern them if it didn't know or understand them?

Mom and Dad's lawyer said, "Ashley was born with a narrow vagina and an enlarged clitoris."

"It's not a clitoris," I said. "It has a foreskin. I pee from it. It stands up when I'm turned on and goes soft again when I'm done."

"Ashley, honestly!" Evie's lawyer hissed.

What? I couldn't just sit back and let other people tell lies about me. Especially when those lies were helping to get my big sister in trouble.

"You people just want to shove me into a box," I said. "Why can't you leave me alone? I'm a boy. I don't want to wear a dress, I don't want my penis chopped off, and I don't want to have kids. I want to live with my sister. *She* doesn't make me feel bad for being born the way I was."

The judge looked uncomfortable. "Perhaps this aspect of the argument should be settled out of court."

But this wasn't just an aspect of the argument; it was the whole argument. He didn't understand. He couldn't empathize because he couldn't begin to understand. I felt my heart sinking into my stomach.

"I'm not a girl," I said, taking out the photocopy of my birth certificate. I'd folded it up so I could stick it in my pocket. As soon as I opened it, Mom sat up like a dog on point. She actually leaned partway across the table to snatch it out of my hands, staring at it like it was a witch's sigil.

"This—this isn't—it doesn't mean—" she stammered. "It's a mistake! We meant to correct this ages ago."

"Transitioning without a parent's approval is not legal, Your Honor," her sycophant of a lawyer agreed.

"I didn't transition!" I yelled. "I was always a boy!"

"Let's have a recess," the judge said. "I think I may need a consult on this."

We all left the room for a break. I went downstairs to the lobby with Evie and Trina. We sat on one of the hard, plastic benches by the vending machines while Evie tried to pick a candy bar to buy—like that was her biggest problem in the world right now. I kind of admired her composure.

I heard heels on the floor behind us, smelled Mom's sickly sweet perfume, and then saw her when she stepped in my way, filling my field of vision.

"I wish you wouldn't fight us on this," she insisted shakily.

I looked up at her, tired. "Why are you doing this, Mom?"

"I'm trying to make you normal," she said. "You don't realize it right now, but you're ruining your life!"

"How am I ruining my life? I just want to live the way I was born!"

"Don't you understand?" she said tightly. "There's no place in the world for people like you!"

"Bet you wish you'd had an amnio done now, huh?" I asked. "Had me aborted, like your mom did one of your siblings?"

"What?"

"You didn't know that, did you? What was it, she was too ashamed to tell you? It's true, Mom. You had a brother or a sister who was intersex, and your mom found out about it when they were still an embryo. She couldn't stand having a freak in the picture. So they got rid of it."

"That's not . . . that was never . . . she would never . . ."

"That's what you would've done to me if you'd known, isn't it? But you didn't know ahead of time. So instead you think you can disguise me, maybe, make me look a different way, so nobody who looks at me even knows what they're seeing. But you wouldn't have to worry about me if you'd *just let me go!*"

I had so much more I wanted to say to her. I didn't care that my voice was rising in volume, that people walking behind us could probably hear snippets of our conversation. But unfortunately, the recess was over. We had to go back in the courtroom and play the semantics game all over again.

◆◆◆

Things could never just be easy with Mom and Dad. Instead of concluding proceedings right then and there, Judge Tsang decided we were going to have to go home and come back again in late August. I wanted to scream.

I slept fitfully that night, and in the morning, I felt so restless, so agitated, that I had to do something, even if it was a bad idea.

I called my mother to talk.

"Why do you hate me, Mom?" I asked the moment she picked up.

"I don't hate you, Ashley," Mom said. "You're the one who's making our lives so hard! Please—"

"You hate me," I said, sitting on the bed in Evie's office. "You have to. If you loved me, you wouldn't keep hurting me like this. You'd let me live here in Boston. You'd leave me alone."

"You're my baby," she said thickly. I could hear in her voice that she'd started crying.

"Mom, stop." I was tired of having to comfort her when I was the one who needed support.

"And saying all those terrible things to me—that I would have a-aborted you—"

"Uncle Henry told me you were going to have surgery done on me, but he talked you out of it."

"That was just to m-make it easier on you! It's so hard, living this way!"

"You don't need to tell me! I'm the one who has to live it! Why do you keep acting like you have a damn clue what this is like?"

She went silent. A creeping suspicion started to sink in.

In looking for a relative of mine who might be intersex, I'd missed the most obvious one.

"Grandma didn't get an abortion," I said. "Did she? *You're* the one who's intersex."

"Oh God," Mom said on a rattling breath. "Oh God . . ."

"You are. You're intersex!"

"Be quiet! Please!"

I quieted down, even though I was alone in the room.

"They shaved my p-penis down," she stammered meekly. "They rerouted my urethra so I could go to the bathroom the way girls do."

"That's why you have so many UTIs," I said, thinking of Ariel and all their infections.

"She said we can't tell, so please! Don't tell!"

It felt like a monster was pressing down on my shoulders with heavy paws; my knees were buckling; the soft earth was sinking underneath me to swallow me up. Sadness really was a heavy thing. Because I could see now that Mom wasn't ignorant, like Evie had thought, or even spiteful, like I had. She was traumatized.

"Mom," I said. "You went through all that, and you *still* don't understand why I'm pushing back?"

"Of course I understand! Don't you think I was angry with my mom too? Don't you think I h-had arguments with her when I was your age?"

"Then why?"

"Because I know now that she was right!" she said, strangled.

"No, you don't," I said. "You've convinced yourself she was right, because that way it becomes your fault you're unhappy, not hers."

"I could never have married your father if she hadn't modified me." Yeah, that much checked out; Dad must not know. She really hadn't told *anyone*. "I could never have lived like a normal woman!"

"You could have had the choice," I said. "Somebody took it from you. And now you're trying to take it from me. You're trying to punish me the way you were punished. Because misery loves company, right?"

I tried to imagine dating someone, marrying someone, having kids with that person, all the while knowing that if they ever found out about a fundamental aspect of your biology, they'd react the way Louisa Carmichael had reacted to me. I tried to imagine sitting at family gatherings, knowing the vile things your own siblings would call you if they knew. And then I tried to imagine willingly putting someone else through the same ordeal.

"Did you ever wonder, Mom? You said you argued with your mother when you were my age. That means a part of you wondered what it could have been like. Maybe a part of you wondered if you were really a boy, or something in-between. Or if you could've still been a girl even without getting *modified*. Maybe you liked playing with Tonka trucks and eating worms when you were little. Maybe you met a girl in school, a girl who gave you funny feelings . . ."

"Don't say that!" She was practically screaming with fright; I had to wonder whether Dad was home, to hear her carrying on like this.

"And another thing," I said, thinking about Michelle. "You're a racist, Mom. But that's something else I don't know how to fix."

I was tired. Like, bone-deep tired. I wanted to be awake later in the evening for the InterPersonal meeting. I hung up with her, rubbed my eyes, and curled up on the bed for a nap.

It was messed up, I'm sure, but a part of me wished I could go home right now—just for a little while, to tell my mom that I was here for her, and everything was going to be all right.

❧ ❧ ❧

When I went to meet with the support group that night, I saw there were two new members, a chubby Asian boy around Airy's age and a white woman in her sixties who called everybody "darling" and thought everything was "magnificent." She was so affectionate that I had to dodge cheek kisses from her before I'd even told her my name.

Everyone went around saying how their week had gone. During a lull in the conversation, I happened to bring up what I'd learned about my mother. I asked everyone what they thought I should do about it.

"For starters," Ariel said, stretching their legs, "you shouldn't have told us. She obviously didn't want anybody to know."

"Well, yeah," I said sheepishly, "but she's using her issues to give *me* issues."

Ted heaved a sigh. "I don't know what you can really do except hang in there until you turn eighteen and become a legal adult. It's going to be a long time before the law catches up with us."

So what? In the meantime, we were stuck occupying the fringes of society, waiting for people to cotton on to the fact that we were real? Where did that get us? If we couldn't even walk in some stupid Fourth of July parade, there wasn't a whole lot we could do to tell people we were here.

"Although," Ted said, "maybe you could invite your mother to join the support group too. Maybe when she sees how many of us there are, it'll open her mind a little bit."

"I don't know," I said. "She was pretty adamant that I shut up about it. I think her worst fear is that my dad finds out."

"Poor woman."

"Not poor woman," said Ariel, annoyed, even though they were the one who'd just stuck up for my mom's right to privacy. "She's a grown-up. She should pull herself together and act like one, for her kid's sake. Just because she was abused doesn't mean she had a right to abuse somebody else."

"Abuse?" I laughed uncomfortably. It sounded kind of dramatic.

"That's what she's done to you," Ariel said matter-of-factly. "She tried to make you into someone you're not. Doesn't matter if she said she did it out of love. Doesn't matter if she's been hurt too. It's abuse."

I fell silent. I'd always thought of abuse as something that happened to defenseless little kids. Not me. But maybe Ariel had a point—although I didn't really want to admit it.

The others kept up the discussion for a while, going all big-picture and philosophical and psychoanalytic, but it didn't do me any good. If even these people didn't have any answers for me, I didn't see how I was supposed to come up with one myself.

◆◆◆

But I did, the very next day.

Evie and Trina had both left the apartment for work. Not wanting to be alone, I'd taken a trip to the West End Museum to watch Ariel in action. Well, and to annoy them by making ridiculous faces. They pretended not to notice me when they were giving a tour to a group of visitors, but I could see I'd been successful every time they gnashed their teeth.

The exhibits were pretty interesting. There were grainy, black-and-white childhood photos of Leonard Nimoy, who had lived in the neighborhood before its destruction; pieces of rubble from immigrant-run restaurants, now long defunct; even a panorama of the old Boston skyline. I thought the museum served as a warning to never again let greed overtake human compassion. But I wasn't kidding myself. Greed was always going to win out in the end, just like it had done for old Judge Corwin. Funny thing was, I didn't know why. You couldn't take your riches with you to the grave.

I used the museum's bathroom—the men's room, not the ladies'. It was there that I realized how I was going to get Mom to back off, once and for all. I hated the thought of what I was about to do, but then I reminded myself that Mom hadn't felt any guilt for the entire year that she was forcing me to masquerade as somebody I wasn't. If she didn't feel guilty, I didn't have to, either.

I sent her a quick text message, knowing she was probably at work. Ariel finished their shift around four o'clock and took me upstairs with them to their apartment—"Because I can't think of any other way to get rid of you, and you standing there like an ugly ape is bad for business." I didn't know about Trina, but Evie was going to be late to come home today. Ariel said I was free to have dinner with them. "But it's going to be kosher, so deal with it. And don't even think about asking me for milk."

Mom texted me back while I was in the middle of rolling my eyes. **what is it?** she had written.

I cut straight to the point. **let me live with evie and trina, or i'm telling dad you're intersex.**

It was several long minutes before she responded. **he won't believe that**

i can just show him this conversation.

The phone started ringing. I answered it, listening to Ariel in the kitchen, cursing the spitting oil for burning their hand.

"Why are you doing this?" Mom asked fearfully.

"Because you don't care about me," I said. "You only care about you. So if I can't get you to leave me alone for my sake, I'll get you to do it for your own sake."

"He won't believe you." Her voice was quavering. "I didn't admit to anything."

"You don't think he'll get suspicious once I plant the seed in his head? Maybe he'll insist you get yourself tested. You do that, and it's going to show up. What's he going to think when he finds out he isn't married to a woman?"

Every word coming out of my mouth made me feel like the most terrible person on earth. There was no getting around that. But I had to do this. Mom might say she loved me and wanted what was best for me, but in reality she had done everything in her power to hurt me. I had to get her to stop.

Mom was already begging me not to say a word. I could hear the hollow ringing in her voice that told me she was only minutes away from crying. It felt sick and wrong to have this much power over her. Over anyone.

"Ashley?" Mom said brokenly. "Please?"

I gripped the phone in one hand, wishing in spite of myself that I could hug her. "Don't worry, Mom," I said. "I will keep silent."

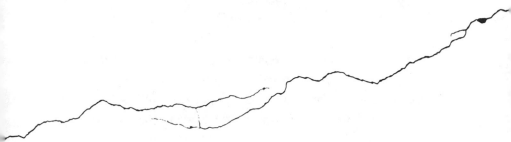

22

I saw Bridget Bishop's photo in a history textbook when I was in seventh grade. It was a colorized artist's rendition, but it was said to be based on contemporary accounts—not just of the clothes she would have worn and the way she would have kept her hair, but what her face supposedly looked like, as described by her children and peers. I remembered thinking that in the image, she looked far too saintly to be a witch. She had a milky, rounded, heart-shaped face with a widow's peak, kind of like Dad's; small lips; a long nose; and big, chocolate-colored eyes you could have fallen into. In the drawing, she was smiling serenely, even as the judge's men led her along the road with a rope around her wrists, like some kind of prize pig. Her dark hair with its split ends hung freely around her shoulders. After her accusation, she wouldn't have been considered a woman of modesty, so she wouldn't have needed to wear the customary bonnet.

I didn't know how much of that drawing was accurate and how much was just revisionism. I always pictured that Bridget Bishop was an older, more worldly woman. I mean, she owned and operated two taverns. She proudly wore red, the color of sin. And by the time she was tried and executed for something she didn't do, she'd already been married three times. To me, the likelihood that she looked anything like the girl in the drawing was low.

I think that people, especially people who get coded as female, have to present themselves a certain way if they want to be seen as sympathetic. Making Bridget Bishop look like a pretty little ingenue made it more of a tragedy that she was murdered. Why? She could have been a floozy and an adulterer, for all I cared. She could have been the nastiest fucking bitch on the planet, or an ugly old crone. Or she could have been an actual witch, the kind who danced at midnight and worshiped trees. She still wouldn't have deserved to die.

When I got my period, when I started feminizing, I lost my say over how I was perceived. From then on, I had to look and behave a certain way—or worse, aspects of my personality that had always been there suddenly had the words "for a girl" tacked on at the end. "You're so strong . . . for a girl." "You know so much about soccer . . . for a girl."

And possibly the most bizarre part? Some of the most judgmental people had been girls at Samuel Parris Private Academy, the ones who chose to believe Tyler's version of events over mine. Like, at what stage in life did girls get taught to rip one another to shreds? How was this so ingrained in our society that it was taken for granted at this point?

Don't get me wrong. Guys could be shitty, especially when it came to gay panic. But for the most part, we tended to have one another's backs. There was a reason "the bro code" was a thing, for instance.

Here's where it gets even more bizarre. When people went back to seeing me as a guy, the qualifiers all disappeared without fanfare. I wasn't strong and cool and funny "for a guy."

I was going to have to work overtime now to keep my secret from getting out again. Because once people knew your genitals included a vagina, those genitals were no longer yours to control. I couldn't speak for other intersex guys, but a lot of the grief I'd gotten over the past year was because my body committed the unpardonable sin of being part female.

I didn't think it was a coincidence that only seven of the twenty-four witch trial victims were guys. The most famous of the men convicted was named Giles Corey. He was that badass guy I mentioned earlier who got crushed to death— the one who cried "More weight!" when he was lying under so many rocks that his tongue and eyes were bulging out of his head.

In 1712 the State of Massachusetts posthumously absolved Giles Corey of all wrongdoing. His wife, Martha, was never pardoned.

◆◆◆

Evie's final court date was toward the end of the month. Now that I knew it was such a lax environment, I didn't bother dressing up. When we went in the courtroom, Mom and Dad weren't there. Their lawyer was, and he explained that our parents had had a change of heart and thought it might be a good idea for me to stay with Evie for a while. They thought, he said, that getting to live in a big city for a few years would broaden my horizons. And they wanted me to have a good relationship with my sister. They were dropping all charges against her, as long as she consulted with them for major medical decisions.

I rolled my eyes so hard, I don't know how they didn't fall out of my head. Everybody shook hands, but I kept mine to myself. Ariel had told me the other night that evil spread through the world through touch. I wasn't sure I believed that, but I wanted to keep my chances low.

"How did you do that?" Evie asked.

She and I were walking away from the courthouse to Beacon Hill. I wanted to show her that cool old cobblestone street I'd found the day of her first hearing.

"I dunno," I said carefully. I remembered what Ariel had said, that maybe Mom wouldn't want people knowing so much about her. I didn't want to cause her more harm or pain than I already had, if I could avoid it. "Mom and Dad must have gotten tired of riding the train out here every few weeks."

Evie shook her head, which was her way of smiling. She must be relieved. I knew I was—for her more than anything.

When I showed her what Acorn Street looked like, she wasn't as impressed as I'd expected her to be. "Oh, I've seen this before," she said, then took me to a nearby ice cream parlor called JP Licks. I guess it was cool in its own way, with hanging bauble lights that looked like white raindrops. The best part: they had coffee-flavored ice cream. It was like I didn't have to go home to experience being home. I ordered some, and Evie got herself oatmeal cookie frozen yogurt. We ate outside, watching bicyclists and professionals parade down the busy street. I felt comfortable, and wanted, and loved. The witch in me was laid to rest.

◆◆◆

All through the end of August, Evie took me to different public schools to see which ones I might like best. There were more than a hundred in Boston, so obviously we couldn't visit them all. We stuck mostly to the area around the Financial District. There was one toward the bottom of the North End I thought was pretty cool. It was called Freedom Hill High School, and at a glance, it looked like the apartment buildings on either side of it: three stories with a big red entrance like a sawed-off barn door. The principal arranged to show us around a few days before the semester began. I wasn't sold for sure until Principal Morris said they had a soccer team. I knew then and there that they needed me.

We didn't have an official supply list yet, but Evie decided we had better get a couple of notebooks and pens. She took me to a drugstore not far from her apartment building to get binders, erasers, even white-out. She was overdoing it, I thought, never having been responsible for a younger human being before.

"Hey," I said, when we were checking out. "Good practice for whenever you guys adopt Zelda and Link."

"Those are not going to be their names."

"Mario and Peach. Okay."

"Just stop. Don't make me regret being related to you by blood."

◆◆◆

I woke early for my first day of school. I dressed quickly and dragged my ass into the kitchen. Evie and Trina didn't need to be awake for an hour or more, so I was on my own, but I didn't mind. It meant I'd have some time alone with my thoughts.

I remembered my first day of school with Michelle and Corey a year ago, how disappointed I'd been to learn how few classes I had with either one of them. I thought how different my life would have been right now if class scheduling had been the worst of my disappointments that year. Probably I'd be getting ready to go back to Lawson with the two of them. I felt a strange longing for the life I might have lived in another universe.

It wasn't like we deliberately set out to part ways. Reality forked at every decision we made, carrying some people farther away from us than others. It was sad, not least because all we could do was let it.

I ate soggy cornflakes while checking the news on my cell phone, then packed my shit and headed out the door. Now that I had a student pass, I thought it would be fun to take the train. Something about riding it made me feel united with the groggy humans around me. I surveyed the passengers and counted two redheads amid a sea of black and brown. I saw a man with thick specs and suspenders, a boy with sagging shorts, a fifty-year-old woman in a sparkling tutu. I wondered which one of them was hiding a secret like mine.

I got off the train and trekked up the slope to Freedom Hill High. There were so many people trying to get through the doors at the same time that it caused a minor traffic jam. Finally I edged my way inside. I didn't feel like going straight to homeroom—which was on the second floor—so I spent some time locating my locker and figuring out the combination. Nobody was staring at me funny, or even looking twice at me. It came as a huge relief.

"Ash? Hi, Ash!"

Thomas Demaine ran down the hall toward me, waving. He knocked into a couple of our classmates along the way, but they didn't seem to mind.

"You go to school here?" I asked, grinning.

"I'm a junior," Thomas said. "Wow, this is great—now I don't have to look for somebody to sit with at lunch."

I'd almost forgotten he was a transplant, like me.

We talked for a while about the Skeletronics, which I'd gotten him to listen to during our last InterPersonal meeting. The first warning bell rang. I thought I might need some time to find my classroom, so we said goodbye, and I went up the stuffy staircase to the second floor. A girl stopping at the drinking fountain blocked my way but said sorry. I went around her.

Homeroom had a peculiar configuration, the students' desks all arranged in a giant semicircle, leaving an empty space in the middle of the room. I picked an empty desk and sat down, tucking my book bag between my feet. It wasn't long before the seats on either side of me started filling out.

"Hey, man," said a guy to my left.

"Hey," I said.

We found out why the desks were set up that way when the physics teacher, Mr. Nallaparaju, started walking among them while he lectured. Apparently he was the kind who didn't like to sit idle. He told us physics was the study of "how things work—how everything works." I opened my notebook and marked the page with today's date.

"And just so you know," Mr. Nallaparaju said, "*all* things can be explained by physics if you break them down to their tiniest components. For example, the witch trials in our neighboring town of sleepy little Salem. It all started with a little ice age . . ."

My phone buzzed quietly in my pocket. I waited until his back was turned, then pulled it out, hiding it under my desk. I opened my texts.

i'm still here.

I didn't understand, or not at first. The message before that one—which had apparently been sent by me—was time-stamped all the way back to April 27.

I looked at the top of the screen, where I saw Michelle's name.

Now I didn't care whether I got caught. My fingers flew across the keyboard. My eyes were blurry and my temples felt tight and my heart was racing too fast in my chest. I wrote: **what happened? WHAT HAPPENED? please tell me you're okay!**

Speech bubble. She was typing back.

do you know i learned horseback riding, ash? yes, i am 100% serious, like apparently gay people don't know how to ride horses?

somebody ought to tell that to alexander the great.

i can make a mean omelet now, too.

I knew this girl inside and out. She always downplayed it when things were bothering her. Right now I was just glad she was alive and cognizant. I started to write back to her when Mr. Nallaparaju said, "Mr. Bishop, is that a hot date you've got there?"

A couple of the people nearest me laughed. He obviously didn't expect anyone to really pay attention on the first day of school, because he went back to rambling about how he wanted to have Michio Kaku's babies or something.

During the couple of minutes between classes, I called Michelle. I just wanted to hear her voice.

"Ash?"

It sounded a little scratchy, but it was hers.

"Christ, Michelle." I started to say a dozen things at once, a confusing jumble of emotions and words. "You don't—are you—"

"I'm with my Uncle Deak," she said, and I could practically hear her shaky smile. "Might have to go back to my parents in a month, but they said they wouldn't send me to that place ever again. He—he was so mad. You should've seen it."

"Are you in Salem right now?"

"Boston. He lives here."

My skin prickled. "You'll never believe this . . ."

We made arrangements to meet up that afternoon. I was so preoccupied with the thought of her, and her face, and her presence, I didn't pay attention at all for the remainder of the school day.

When school let out, I ran back to Evie's apartment and burst through the door so fast, Trina yelled at me. I threw my books down beside the couch—"Are you seriously going to leave those there?"—and raced back down to the lobby. I'd offered to pick her up, but Michelle had said she wanted to meet me here. **To see your sister's bitchin' crash pad, of course.**

Whether it was my imagination, or the fact that I hadn't seen her in four months, Michelle looked much skinnier to me when I laid eyes on her. She was wearing her Skeletronics T-shirt, but practically swimming in it. Her hair was wilder than usual, making me think she hadn't been allowed any of her usual hair care products while at the facility. She seemed almost afraid to approach me; her eyes were very wide behind her glasses. But within a moment, I realized what it was she was seeing: Her eyes kept going from my hair to my chest and back again.

"Just get over here, okay?" I said.

She timidly moved toward me until she was close enough for me to pull her into my arms. She squeaked; I felt her shoulders shaking, and she molded herself against me like she was afraid of what would happen if I let go. I pretended not to notice when my shoulder grew wet, nor when she eventually pulled back to take her glasses off, drying them on her shirt.

Michelle had come back from Indiana with a few new

idiosyncrasies. She kept running her tongue over her front teeth between pauses in conversation. I couldn't understand why she was doing it until I noticed a tiny chip on one that hadn't been there before. I probably wouldn't have seen it had I not been hyperaware of her lips and tongue.

"You wanna come inside?" I asked.

"No," she said. "I—I've been inside a lot. I just want to be outside some."

"I know a place you'd really like. Wanna go see it?"

"Okay, Ash," she said softly. She tucked her small hand into mine.

I took her to Beacon Hill, then down the road to Acorn Street. It was empty and quiet. There was a sweet smell to the air, a mix of cut grass and still water. Michelle looked around us, and I knew she was appreciating the place the same way I had.

"That's real cobblestone," I said. "Even Salem doesn't have a road like it."

"So, this might be the oldest road in America?"

"Maybe. I don't know."

She let go of my hand and sat down on the bumpy path. She flashed me a sweet, absent little smile. I sat down with her. The rocks were warmed by the sun, but cooled by the shade of the alley. They felt comfortable under my thighs.

"Michelle," I began. "If you don't want to tell me, you don't have to. But . . . are you okay? Were you hurt?"

Michelle shrugged, dodging the question at first. Then she said, "They were in a weird position, with me, because I said from the start that I was straight. I was in love with a boy, that is. So they didn't really know what to do to correct me, because I was already corrected? But the way they treated the other kids there . . ."

Her eyes filled up with tears again. She tilted her head back so they couldn't fall; she wiped at her lashes where they had gone moist at the corners. She righted her head again.

"It was evil," she said simply. "Locking people in small, dark rooms for hours until they apologized for something they had said, or making them look at naked pictures of the opposite sex—I just don't know how you can do that to a person and that's okay."

"It's not," I said. "But what can we do? I mean, how can we change it? How can we change any of it?" It wasn't a rhetorical question. I was open to ideas.

"Ash!" Michelle said, sitting up straight.

"What?"

"Let's become witches for real," she said.

I looked at her and saw she was at least partly serious.

"You want to?" I said. I didn't believe in witchcraft, but I was willing to try anything for her. And in the long run, trying something beat doing nothing.

Michelle grinned shakily. The more she looked at me, the more her smile evened itself out. In that moment I thought things would be okay.

"We'll go to that old witchcraft store back home," Michelle said. "Learn a spell big enough that we can cast it on the whole world, and it'll make people treat each other right. Even if they don't want to."

"Altruistic mind control," I said. "I like it."

"You promise me we'll do this?"

"Promise," I said.

We went back to Salem that weekend, Michelle and I. We visited Crow Haven Corner, bought a couple of candles and spell books and even a novel about Dorcas Good. On Saturday, we officially created our coven: the Contemporary Witches of

Salem. It was just the two of us for now, but I thought I might convince her to let Thomas and Ariel and the others join up. We could use the numbers, I argued, if we wanted to attempt a spell as big as the one she had in mind.

In the privacy of my bedroom, we lit a pink candle and practiced a love spell. I worried it would cancel itself out, since we were already in love, but Michelle told me there was no need for concern. The more of it you gave, she said, the more of it you had. "And I think we're going to need a lot of it. It's just a feeling."

AUTHOR'S NOTE

"Intersex" encompasses a broad spectrum of genital and chromosomal conditions that fall outside the accepted sex binary. While we assign terms to many of these conditions, like congenital adrenal hyperplasia and androgen insensitivity syndrome, these names do not dictate how the conditions must behave. Rather, they are medical professionals' best attempts at assigning a recognizable name to the assortment of symptoms affecting the patient. New intersex conditions are being discovered to this day. Some intersex individuals don't even have a name for the condition they were born with. Others still might be assigned one condition at birth, only to discover later on that they present symptoms of another.

The growing medical consensus is that sex and gender are a spectrum. Problems will always arise when society tries to assign a binary to a spectrum.

Ash Bishop is an intersex boy diagnosed with stage II congenital adrenal hyperplasia at birth. He has XX chromosomes, a hypospadic microphallus, a working ovary, and a nonfunctional testicle (an atypical gonadal configuration, but documented in at least six CAH patients since the 1980s). In adolescence, Ash's diagnosis is amended to POR deficiency, a specific type of CAH where salt wasting and other problems develop later in life rather than infancy. Bone development is sometimes, but not always, malformed.

While most XX-CAH babies are assigned female at birth on doctors' recommendations, some are assigned male based on their parents' wishes. Thanks to insufficient records, we do not know how common this is worldwide.

Many intersex people and allies have advocated against surgeries to alter the genitalia of intersex children before they are old enough to consent. But this long-standing practice continues, as do misconceptions about intersex conditions.

Our bodies are unusual, beautiful, and constantly challenging the rigid world we were born in. They do not deserve to be mutilated or stigmatized merely because they make some people uncomfortable.

ACKNOWLEDGMENTS

My thanks go to the following medical researchers for their insights: doctors Shilpa Sharma and Devendra K. Gupta of the All India Institute of Medical Sciences; Drs. Lei Zhang, Linda D. Cooley, Sonal R. Chandratre, Atif Ahmed, and Jill D. Jacobson of the Children's Mercy Hospital of Kansas City; and Dr. Jan Idkowiak, Ms. Deborah Cragun, Dr. Robert Hopkin, and Dr. Wiebke Arlt of the University of Washington.

Thanks to interAct for providing intersex children with the resources and support they need to navigate their unique conditions. Thanks also to Pidgeon Pagonis, Sean Saifa Wall, Hida Viloria, Anunnaki Ray Marquez, and so many other inspirational intersex speakers who have the courage to speak out about the way they and others have been and are still being treated. I don't know how you do it.

Thanks to my beta readers, friends, and family; to Laura Strachan, for believing in this book when I sometimes didn't; and to Amy Fitzgerald, for being a patient angel and an awesome editor.

Thank to Lily, aka "Hot Cookie"—you know who you are. And thanks to you for reading this far.

QUESTIONS FOR DISCUSSION

1. After Ash gets his period, why do you think people start assuming he's a girl?

2. How does Ash feel when people misgender him and pressure him to present as a girl?

3. When people perceive Ash as a girl, how do they treat him differently than they would treat a guy? Consider Corey, Tyler, and Naia.

4. What parallels does Ash see between himself and Salem's accused witches in the 1690s?

5. What does Michelle tell Ash about her experience as one of the few Black people in Salem? How is this similar to and different from Ash's experience as an intersex guy?

6. What does Ash learn from attending InterPersonal meetings? What is something he discovers that surprised you as a reader?

7. Compare Ariel's feelings about being intersex to Thomas's. Why do you think their relationships with their bodies are so different?

8. How do you feel about the way Ash ultimately gets his mother to drop the custody battle? If you were in Ash's position, what do you think you would do?

9. Ariel tells Ash that Ash's parents have been abusive, a label that surprises Ash. What are some examples of his parents' emotional and psychological abuse? How is his mother's abuse different from his father's?

10. What do you think of Ash's reflection that "a lot of the grief I'd gotten over the past year was because my body committed the unpardonable sin of being part female"?

ABOUT THE AUTHOR

Sol Santana is an intersex author, a preschool teacher in training, and a lover of wildlife who aims to promote empathy through her work. *Just Ash* is her first novel.